Horror in the night

Jenny crept soundlessly through the dark towards the cabin, towards the unknown man who was spraying it with gasoline. Inside, Colly and Sandro were sitting—both of them battered and crippled—unaware of the flaming pyre being prepared for them.

Jenny drew silently closer to the arsonous enemy. Crouched and waited. Then she jumped in a flat dive and the fingers of her left hand jabbed into his eye!

"Mr. Drummond has a suave ingenuity that is irresistible, and his timing, or pacing, is flawless."   —*The New Yorker*

"A lively new thriller series . . . most exciting."   —*Publishers' Weekly*

THE POWER
OF
THE BUG

Ivor Drummond

PYRAMID BOOKS NEW YORK

THE POWER OF THE BUG

A PYRAMID BOOK

Published by arrangement with St. Martin's Press, Inc.

Copyright © 1974 by Ivor Drummond

Pyramid edition published August 1975

ISBN 0-515-03796-6

Printed in the United States of America

Pyramid Books are published by Pyramid Communications, Inc. Its trademarks, consisting of the word "Pyramid" and the portrayal of a pyramid, are registered in the United States Patent Office.

Pyramid Communications, Inc.,
919 Third Avenue, New York, N.Y. 10022

CHAPTER ONE

The Cordle summer place in Vermont was planned in 1911. It was completed just before Europe erupted in a war which the Cordles regarded as none of their business.

The estate was about the biggest and grandest in the state. Vermont runs, on the whole, to unostentatious properties of moderate size. It was considered an odd choice by old James Cordle's contemporaries. They thought it characteristic of his crusty eccentricity. They mostly spent their summers on Long Island. Some went to Newport; some joined the Bostonians on Cape Cod, or even ventured right up the North East to Bar Harbor. None built summer palaces, in wastes of mountains, far inland in Vermont. There was no point to it. The place just had blueberries and balsam and bare rocks and a few streams and ponds. The local farmers were wry and independent. They were unimpressed by New York millionaires. They did not tug their forelocks. The summer visitors were Harvard professors and the like, men with small bank balances and radical opinions. But James Cordle ignored the astonishment of his acquaintances, acquired a huge acreage of useless mountain land, and built his palace.

James despised the decadent aristocracies of Europe, as well as those of Virginia and Louisiana. Therefore he modeled neither his palace nor his life-style on theirs. The house rambled down the side of a mountain. It resembled a village pushed together by a giant playing with building blocks, so that detached houses, of widely differing sizes and architectural styles, were stuck together instead of separate, and formed a single incongruous jumble. Some of the materials were local, some brought at terrifying expense from far away. When new, the house must have been the ugliest in America.

Sixty years mellowed it. The mountainside became used to the house, and the house to the mountainside. Such trees and creepers as withstood the Vermont winter shrouded parts of it. Generations of imported gardeners created delightful, half-wild gardens, with precipitous walks and splendid mountain vistas. James Cordle's son and grandson improved on his design. They painted here, added there, demolished elsewhere. Most important, an amiable tradition grew up that the house was always full all summer. Nephews, nieces, cousins and friends arrived, usually with children. The many families often spent their days apart, but always their evenings together. Spruce Ledge became all summer a relaxed and cheerful community, with low standards of dress and high standards of manners. The sound of a string quartet was as probable as the sound of a pop group, the click of chessmen as the ping of tennis-balls.

David Cordle, James's grandson, could not be prized away from Spruce Ledge from the beginning of June until the end of September. As a boy he had spent all his summers there, because there was nowhere else he wanted to go. As a young man, he had to prove himself in the network of family businesses. He could only allow himself an occasional week in Vermont. But every night and morning in New York in the summer he ached for his mountains: for the bare granite, the balsamy smells, the clean air, and the cheerful, cultured community of Spruce Ledge. Now that he was 55, and Board Chairman, he could please himself.

Not that his control of the Cordle empire slackened while he spent those months in Vermont. He delegated, of course: but nothing happened of importance in any of his companies that he did not know about. He worked most mornings. He brought a small, key staff. They worked all day. Sometimes they joined the family in the evening. On these occasions Dave made them feel like part of the family. Dave's wife Camilla made them feel like servants with dirty fingernails.

Dave woke on the morning of July 2nd and saw that the day was the most beautiful of the summer. He came to the same conclusion when he woke most mornings, as he had a cheerful and optimistic disposition.

He glanced across the big white-painted bedroom at his wife. She was asleep. In sleep, her face lost its cold and formidable expression, and became both older and younger than by day. Older because of the lines and pouches, the sagging flesh unchecked by muscular effort and iron will; younger because of the childlike vulnerability of the sleeper, who cannot, while sleeping, put employees in their places. Dave felt his usual twinge of impatient tenderness. They had been married 28 years. He knew her through and through. She had faults but there was much in her to love. She was a shrewd manager but imperceptive about people. She was not stupid but she was thick-skinned. Of course that was fortunate. It meant she did not know about Dave as Dave knew about her. Had it not been so she must have found him out, must have sensed something strange about him, must have guessed at the part of his life that nobody knew about, nobody at all, except himself and Geoff.

Dave pulled on swimming trunks and walked briskly to the pool. The sun was just up over the lip of the mountains. The morning was clear and absolutely windless. Dave's figure was excellent for a man of his age. He arrived at the edge of the pool. It gave him pleasure, as always. Although it was heated and filtered, it resembled as far as possible a natural mountain pond, with rocks and bushes to the edge. Visitors said that it was the most beautiful pool in America and they were right.

Dave stood on the diving board and looked around. It was old Geoff's favorite place in the world—Geoffrey Cordle, his cousin. Geoff used to stand here on the end of the diving board where Dave now stood, looked around as Dave was now looking, and say there was no place in the world he would rather be. But that was not quite true. There was one other place. Poor Geoff. A little money of his own from his mother, and never did anything to increase it. Loafed for 60 years. A wasted life and a stupid, unnecessary death. Just another victim of the roads, of a drunken teenager at the wheel of a borrowed car. Geoff would be missed in New York, at his club and at concerts and musical parties. He was missed up here at Spruce Ledge. He was missed most of all by Dave.

Everybody knew that Dave missed his gentle, rather precious cousin. But nobody knew how much and nobody knew why.

Dave sliced into the water and swam three lengths of the pool. He climbed out, wiped his hands on the towel, and lit a denicotinized cigarette. He walked back to the house swinging his towel. Birds and insects were busy and vociferous, but no people were about this early. That's why it had been their time, his and Geoff's, to go, before or after a swim, to the old hay store above the stables. It was perfectly safe there, solid, soundproof, unseen. They kept what they needed in a wooden box with a padlock. Dave had the box taken away three weeks ago, immediately they had the news of Geoff's death. Everything in it was destroyed, incinerated. There wasn't a single trace left. The slate was wiped absolutely clean. Never again. Nothing like it for Dave ever again, not without Geoff.

Dave went to his dressing room and shaved and dressed. He brushed his hair carefully. Geoff had always liked his hair. Dave brushed his hair the way Geoff liked it.

Geoff's death was a horrible shock, an irreparable loss, and an overwhelming relief. As long as Geoff was alive there it would be, their secret game, in a secret compartment of Dave's life. Only here at Spruce Ledge, and only in the old hay store. It had begun when Dave was 13 and Geoff 18. Maybe somebody had taught Geoff about it. Geoff taught Dave about it. They borrowed the clothes from people in the house. The clothes went back and nobody noticed. Later they got clothes of their own and kept them in the wooden box with the padlock. The years went by and still they went on. Part of Dave hated it, part wanted it. He grew up, had girls, got married, and still it went on. A few times Dave said no, no more, never again, but the resolution never stuck. It went on. They did it whenever Geoff was at Spruce Ledge for part of the summer.

Of course it harmed nobody. If it was degrading it was not evil because it harmed nobody. But always, always, there was the chance of being found out. There was a tiny terror of somebody getting to know about it. Dave had lived with the terror for 42 years, since the first time they did it when he was 13. Now the terror was over because Geoff was dead.

8

The rest of his life was so good. He had worked hard to make his life a good one and he had succeeded. He had built a big fortune into a bigger one without a single transgression. He was a ruler, wise and temperate but authentically powerful. The whole complex empire was led by him in a very personal sense. He was known to all the people that his companies employed and to a good many of the stockholders. He was held in respect and trust and admiration, all of which he deserved, all of which he had earned.

But if people had found out about Geoff? The companies would have survived, of course. But not with him at their head. The other directors would have eased him out. Certain to have done so. Right to have done so. Because he would never again have been held in any personal respect, never again admired in quite the same way, never again truly trusted.

Outside of his business, Dave had given time, effort and money to many causes. He had been a loyal friend. Many of his benefactions were anonymous. Many of his beneficiaries never knew who saved them from despair. Others knew, and, knowing, told. People went to Dave for money. If they made a good case they got it. It had to be a good case. He was not a sucker. They also went for other kinds of help, and for advice. People Dave had advised often came to him again, for advice on other things.

If he was found out, nobody would ever come to him again for advice. For money, yes. People who wanted money would go anywhere. But he would never again be credited with sanity, maturity, wisdom, goodness if people knew about Geoff. Now they would never know because Geoff was dead and everything was burned in the incinerator.

Dave's marriage had been happy. He had held his wife's love. He had never stepped out of line with other women. His two sons were thoroughly promising. They had plenty of friends and plenty of invitations, but they always wanted to come to Spruce Ledge for their vacations. They brought friends with them, and the friends went away better friends.

And if people had known all about him? There would have been no divorce, nothing messy or hysterical. Camilla would have stood by him. His sons would have defended him to their friends, with their fists if necessary. But the look in their eyes. The aghast murmurs, among them all, behind his back. The sick sense of outrage and betrayal, the pitying disgust. Now he was safe from all that. He was whole and clean. At last he truly deserved the devotion of his family and friends.

Dave missed his cousin, and mourned him, and thanked God that he was dead.

He went down to breakfast. Four young nieces were already there. They greeted him with affection. His swim had given him an appetite. He had a good breakfast and a second cup of coffee and another cigarette. Sharp at nine he went to the part of the rambling house which he had turned into offices.

Gloria was by his desk when he came in. She was 42 and the best secretary in the world. There was plenty to be done. They did it calmly and quickly, Dave himself, Gloria, Chuck, Eric and the others, only ten in all, but able with modern communications and Dave's deep knowledge of his business to keep the ship sailing in the right direction.

At noon Dave said, "Anything else?"

Gloria said, "A Mr. Gabetti made an appointment. He sounded kind of funny."

"Why am I seeing him?"

"He's a local man. He says it's urgent and personal."

"That usually means money. Okay, I'll see him."

A car drove by the windows of the office. It stopped on the other side of the house. Presently Mr. Gabetti was brought to the office, and met by Gloria and ushered into Dave's presence. Gloria withdrew.

Dave saw a squat man with an olive-green skin, who wore a pale grey suit and carried a large-brimmed pale grey hat. He looked like an old-fashioned small-time gangster dressed for a family christening. He wore a diamond ring and a silk necktie and his shoes were highly polished. Both his head and his body were pear-shaped, a small pear joined, without benefit of neck, to a larger one.

Mr. Gabetti said: "It's very kind you give me a little of your time, Mr. Cordle. I represent a group of citizens which is trying to do something about the kids in the big cities. Juvenile delinquency. Something, y'know, positive and constructive. We know there's a dozen ways people approach this problem. They start clubs. Different sports they start. They chase the dope-pushers. All that stuff and more. We have a different idea. It ain't new, we don't claim no originality, but we believe it can do more than it has done, make a real difference to a few kids."

"Go on, Mr. Gabetti," said Dave Cordle. His voice was friendly and interested because that was the way he felt. This vulgar little greaseball was a good citizen, a man with a social conscience.

Mr. Gabetti went on: "The trouble with big cities, Mr. Cordle, they *are* big cities. Concrete for ever, noise, dirt, crowds of people. How can a kid from a poor home grow up a good man in all of that? I tried and I know. I come out of a very poor part of Boston. I had me a record by the time I was 17. I got out, came to a small town, made it straight, but I had plenty to get out *of*, you unnerstand me? There's more don't get out, not ever. Things is closed in on them alla time. Streets, buildings, cops on their necks, no air, no *nature*."

"I'm beginning to understand you," said Dave Cordle.

"Yeah. It's pretty obvious. Like I said, it ain't nothing original. Give the kids air and space and show them God's green trees. Get them out on the mountains. Have them work on a farm, or dig gravel, or haul tree trunks, get up a sweat, swim in an ice-cold pond and sleep under the stars, get me? I don't say it's gonna work a miracle every time, Mr. Cordle, but it oughta be given more chances. *You* should unnerstand, having this place."

"I do," said Dave Cordle. "What do you want me to do?"

"Well, naturally, it's money," said Mr. Gabetti.

"Sure. I like what you've been telling me, Mr. Gabetti. I go along with you. I agree it's not likely to work every time, but if it saves one kid it's worth a lot of effort. I'd like to know more about your operation. Maybe I can help in a bigger way than just giving you a check. Maybe I can find room for a few of your kids here. I know farmers around here, the forest service, some summer camps where there's always a few jobs. I'd like to know what you've achieved so far, maybe meet some of the boys, and of course you'll understand that I'll want to look at your accounts."

Mr. Gabetti's expression did not change. He said carefully: "Having a few boys here is a great thought, Mr.

Cordle, and I certainly appreciate the offer. I dunno if it's possible, though. These dead-end kids is pretty rough."

"Well, we can keep it in mind. Can you give me a few case histories? A few figures? How many kids have you actually taken to the country? How long did they stay? Where did they go? What happened to them afterwards? I take it you keep tabs on the kids. You must have records of all this."

"We will have, Mr. Cordle, when we get started."

"Oh I see. I misunderstood you. This is still on the drawing board. Well, that's fair enough. I take it you already have some contributions? The group you represent have dug into their own pockets a little? Can you tell me how much you have in the kitty, how you intend to spend it, and who is the auditor?

"Thing is, Mr. Cordle, our group, we're none of us rich men. We have the idea, but we don't have the dough to do anything about it. There isn't any kitty and there isn't any auditor."

"Okay. Let's take it from there. My auditors can prepare the accounts as soon as there are any, and I'll put the first ante in the kitty. Then we can discuss how to pick the boys and what to do with them."

"That ain't quite how we figure it, Mr. Cordle."

"No?"

"No. We certainly want your conbribution, but we don't require no auditor and we don't require no help running the operation."

Dave Cordle frowned. He said: "This is a funny way to go about getting help with a charity, Mr. Gabetti."

"I guess it is," said the squat man indifferently.

"You have to publish accounts, and some kind of record of what you're achieving. The law requires that. Your contributors will require it too. I certainly will."

"Law won't never hear about this charity, Mr. Cordle. And you're the one and only contributor."

At last Dave Cordle understood. His only excuse for being so slow was that nobody had ever tried anything like this on him before. He said: "This is some kind of shake-down, is it? You don't have any charity. You're not helping any delinquent kids."

"Maybe so, maybe not. I ain't interested in no questions, Mr. Cordle. I need one hundred thousand dollars, paid in a way that don't start a lotta questions. Put it down as a charity and you get the tax-relief, right? We're making it easy, Mr. Cordle."

"Get out of here."

Dave Cordle did not move or raise his voice, but there was in his manner the menace of a fit and athletic man, and the authority of several million dollars.

The sallow, pear-shaped face of his visitor showed no alarm. Mr. Gabetti showed no immediate intention of getting out. He said: "There's things about you you don't want spread all over, Mr. Cordle."

"You're wrong. You can't blackmail me."

"I don't like that word, Mr. Cordle."

"The hell with your taste in words. I say you can't blackmail me. The truth about every aspect of my life is known. Tell lies about me and you're in bad trouble. As a matter of fact you're in bad trouble anyway." Dave pushed a button on his desk. Gloria's head appeared in the door that led to her room. Dave said: "Gloria, get the police here as soon as possible. A crime has just been committed in this office and I'm holding the criminal. Say I'll give them a sworn statement as soon as they get here."

Gloria's eyes widened with amazement. She nodded, awestruck, and the door closed behind her.

Mr. Gabetti said: "If you wanna play rough, Mr. Cordle. But we're not gonna make up lies about you. We don't have to. It's nothing criminal you did. You don't go to jail if it gets around. But, Christ, it's so pathetic I have to laugh." There was no sign of a smile on Mr. Gabetti's heavy opaque face. "You and the old fairy, you go to some room over the garage. I ain't seen it but I got pictures of it, hunnerds of pictures taken every five seconds automatically. They're on microfilm but they blow up pretty good. Also tapes I got, miles of tape, and there ain't any secretary gonna wipe a goddam inch of it. I don't have this stuff with me and I don't have it in town. Friends of mine have it all, so it won't do you no good if you have the whole F.B.I. go through my place. My friends have all the equipment for making big prints and lotsa copies of the tapes. They have a mailing-list, Mr. Cordle, as long as this desk. But we don't hafta make any prints. We can burn the stuff. This is strictly a one-off operation, Mr. Cordle. I don't come back here, get it? Word of honor. But I need

13

that dough. I need it bad and I need it right now, get it?"

The local Police Chief arrived with one other officer in a squad car. They did not use the siren as they curved up the driveway. Gloria met them. She led them immediately into Dave Cordle's office to arrest the criminal.

Dave Cordle was alone.

"False alarm," he said. "The guy's harmless. I misunderstood what he was saying."

"You want him booked, Mr. Cordle?"

"Oh no. I'm very sorry I dragged you fellows all the way up here. Sit down now you're here and tell me how everything goes. Gloria, can you rustle up some coffee? Like a doughnut, Chief? Maybe some cool beer instead of coffee?"

To the police, Mr. Cordle was his unruffled, commanding, likeable self.

But Gloria, with the anxious and accurate eye of love, saw terror.

Dave Cordle exactly followed Mr. Gabetti's instructions about the payment.

It could not come out of his personal account. So large a sum, paid to an unknown charity, would have excited curiosity among the various people who saw his personal checkbook—Gloria, bank officers, accountants. Nor could a checkbook about which there had never been any secret suddenly become a top-secret document without arousing equal curiosity. Dave was forced to agree with Gabetti that neither of them wanted curiosity.

The money could not be paid out of any corporate or trading account. Auditors, treasurers, secretaries, would ask questions to which there were no answers.

It was ironic. A poor man can pay blackmail without anybody knowing about it. As long as he stays out of debt nobody is interested in his checkbook. A millionaire can't. $100,000 was not a crippling sum to Dave Cordle. He could lose it and forget about it. But there was no way he could pay it out secretly with his own money or the money of any of his companies.

It could only be paid out of the Cordle Trust account. The Trust had been formed by Dave's father. It supported many charities, medical and scientific research, missionary

14

work in New Guinea, archeological expeditions, and the restoration of pictures and buildings. By the terms of its incorporation, Dave Cordle, as Senior Trustee, could make payments up to a certain sum on his signature alone to any charitable cause he deemed worthy, provided that he supported the payment with a statement to the other Trustees describing the objects of the charity; this statement doubled as an affidavit for the tax authorities that the recipient was a *bona fide* registered charity, keeping and publishing proper accounts.

Dave Cordle made out the check on the afternoon of July 2nd on one of the special big green Cordle Trust check forms. He made it out to Blue Hill Pilgrims. He put it in an envelope without any other enclosure. He addressed the envelope to Gabetti Bottling Inc., Blue Hill, Vt. Then he wrote out the obligatory statement for his colleagues, signed it, and addressed it to the Secretary of the Cordle Trust, in Park Avenue, for registration and filing. He slipped both envelopes into a pile of outgoing family mail on the table by the front door of the house.

He broke the law for the first time in his life. He committed an offence indictable under federal law and punishable by a prison sentence.

He covered up beautifully. Habit and training held. The cheerful, heterogeneous community of Cordles and their relations and friends saw no change. Camilla, preoccupied by her duties as a hostess and her image as a *grande dame,* saw no change. The morning swim, the hours in the office, the sets of tennis, the vigorous walks over the mountains, the festive dinners, the cultured evenings went on as usual. Dave went on as usual.

But to Gloria's eyes Dave was a changed and a smaller man, and she wondered why.

On July 6th Dave received notification from the Secretariat of the Cordle Trust that a $100,000 check in favor of the Blue Hill Pilgrims had been cleared. His statement, as required by the Articles of the Trust, had been registered and filed, and an attested photocopy had been lodged with the tax authorities. Dave intercepted the letter on his way back from the pool to the house, long before Gloria got to the office.

The episode was closed.

If the truth came out he would be tried. He would be found guilty. He could not possibly pretend that he believed what he said in the affidavit about the Blue Hill Pilgrims. There was no mitigation that would not sound ridiculous in court. He was not likely to be sent to prison. He was likely to be fined for signing a declaration knowing it to be false, with the object of deceiving fellow-trustees and tax officials. He was certain to be ridiculed beyond all bearing for placing himself in such a position. The case would receive immense publicity and his useful life would end.

On July 9th Dave Cordle got a letter among many other letters. It was marked STRICTLY CONFIDENTIAL. Gloria did not open it but she looked at it with alarm and consuming curiosity. The envelope was plain white, long, neither cheap nor very expensive. The name and address were neatly typed on an IBM electric like Gloria's own. The postmark was New York. The envelope was stamped, not franked. There was no printed or written indication of the sender.

She handed it to Dave Cordle when he came into the office after swim and breakfast. Her eyebrows were high with unspoken questions. Dave waited until he was alone before he opened it.

The letter was typed and unsigned. It said:

It has come within our knowledge, more by design than accident, that you have:

(1) Submitted to blackmail by a petty criminal;

(2) Misused Trust funds in order to pay the blackmailer;

(3) Uttered a false attestation in order to conceal the same;

(4) Thus rendered yourself liable to fine, imprisonment, or both, as provided by federal statute, as well as to a degree of general derision which will hurt you more than it hurts us.

Our knowledge in the matter is not only complete but completely documented. The evidence will stand up in any court.

Please address yourself to the task of finding $2,000,000, in a form which can conveniently be delivered to us. We realize that this can not be done overnight. We will accordingly allow you a week, at the end of which period you will receive a further communication.

That was all.

Dave stared at the sheet of white typing paper for a long time. Then he crumpled it and burned it in an ashtray, pulverizing the glowing fragments with the end of a pencil.

He buzzed Gloria and said: "Hold everything for a while. I have to stretch my legs."

Gloria said: "What was that funny letter, Mr. Cordle?"

Dave said: "What letter?"

He strode out of the room, quiet in his soft moccasins.

He went out of the house. The garden was full of butterflies, and the air of the scent of balsam. He disappeared along the ridge of a mountain.

CHAPTER TWO

Coleridge Tucker II sat in the bows of a canoe on Lake Dodge in another part of Vermont. He was fly-fishing for trout, casting inshore from out in the lake, into holes in the bank and under rocks and overhanging trees. In the stern of the canoe, holding a dripping paddle, sat a girl. The brightness of her hair was to Colly's eyes more dazzling than the sun. The blueness of her wide, innocent eyes was to him clearer than the sky and deeper than the waters of the lake. To a stranger it would also have seemed sillier than the silliest water bird.

"Look out, you stupid oaf," said the girl, as Colly's fly-line whispered through the windless air. "You nearly hooked me in the bottom."

Colly Tucker was richer than Dave Cordle, but he looked like someone who would be glad of a menial odd job on a remote part of the Cordle estate. He wore ancient sneakers, dirty khaki pants, and a T-shirt that might have belonged to a stoker of careless habits in a ship infested by moth. He was in his early thirties, of medium height and build and coloring; his face was friendly and unmemorable, his eyes a nondescript green, his hair an untidy thatch of mouse. He cast expertly with a Scottish fly-rod from Sharpes of Glasgow. His white floating line hissed out through the guides as he "shot," and the Lee Wulff fly landed like thistledown inches from the trailing twigs of a dead pine tree.

"Not bad," said the girl in the stern in her high, dispassionate English voice. "I expect the fish will think that's a hand-grenade and die of fright."

"Ah, shut up, you limey cow," said Colly affectionately.

The girl was ten years younger than Colly, and if possible worse dressed. She was barefooted. Her feet were small and very dirty. Her tattered jeans were covered in paint, oil and smears of what looked like blood. Her shirt had lost most of its buttons; she had tied the flaps together with a knot at the waist. The rest of her was as striking and unforgettable as the man was not. The body, readily guessable under the awful clothes, was lithe and magnificent. The face framed by the mane of bright gold hair was not quite classically beautiful, being a little too round, a little too childish, a little snub-nosed: but it was breathtakingly pretty. It was not an intelligent face. The great blue eyes looked frankly retarded. From the heartbreaking curve of the full lips you would not expect to hear words of more than two syllables.

She said in her high, clear, upper-class English voice: "Stop waving that rod for a bit, you selfish pig. Let me have a go. You're flogging the water like a washerwoman."

Colly glanced at her and grinned. She looked good enough to eat—after a scrub—and stupid enough to allow herself to be eaten. He knew, as very few people in the world knew, what marvellous camouflage this was. Her brain was rapid, retentive, and highly-trained. Anyone who tried to eat her would find her very tough indeed.

They changed places. Colly nearly fell in. He grumbled: "I asked you along to paddle my own canoe. That's what *you're* here for."

Lady Jennifer Norrington perched herself in the bows. She flicked the Wulff into the hole under the tree.

They caught a brace of small trout each, and then it was time to think about drinks before lunch. Jenny offered Colly the paddle and her place in the stern. He politely declined. She paddled across to the landing-stage on the other side of the pond. Colly tied up the canoe and they walked up the natural ramp of granite to the cabin at the edge of the woods.

An enormous Italian came out of the cabin to meet them. His face was large, dark, and ugly, but illuminated by eyes of utterly incongruous, brilliant, sapphire blue. His hair was black and stiff, and crinkled like the stuffing of an old horsehair mattress; at the sides it was peppered with grey watchsprings. Shoulders, chest and biceps threatened with every movement to burst his beautiful sky-blue silk shirt. His white duck trousers were from London, his leather sandals from Rome.

He said: "I walked to the village. You must go there to the telephone."

"Off you go, Jenny," said Colly.

"Sandro means you, darling," said Jenny.

"No no. It can't be me. Nobody wants to talk to me. I don't have to go to any village."

"Si, caro," said il conte Alessandro di Ganzarello. "A Mister Franklyn Tucker waits for you to telephone. *E molto importante.* Most extremely urgent."

"Ah well, to be sure, Cousin Frank, *he* wants me, that certainly puts a different complexion on things. Yes sir, if Cousin Frank wants me to call him, why, goddam it, call him I will come hell or high water."

"Who is Cousin Frank?" asked Jenny.

"An old stiff with a face like a lizard and a voice like a jackdaw and a mouth like a rattrap and a mind like a rattrap and a handshake like a rattrap—"

"Belt up," said Jenny.

"Okay. Not another word from me. Only to say, since you asked, that Cousin Franklyn Tucker is kind of head Tucker."

"I thought you were, darling. You always *said* you were."

"Well, I am, primogeniture-wise. But Cousin Frank *makes* like it. He does the work. Pretty unfair arrangement, Cousin Frank thinks. I think so too, actually. He has all the fun, all I have is the money. But I always figure we'd best leave it lay. He does the work better than I would. What in the name of God can Frank want with me, in the middle of July, when I'm way the hell up here trying to teach Jenny to catch trout?"

"Teach your grandmother to suck eggs," said Jenny. "I was catching better trout than these when you were swinging from tree to tree by your tail."

"Kindly leave my tail out of this," said Colly with dignity.

He got into the jeep, nevertheless, and drove the four

20

miles to the village. He telephoned from the Post Office.

Franklyn Tucker's voice came nasal and distorted from New York. "Want you to represent the family at David Cordle's funeral."

Over Colly's strenuous objections, Cousin Frank reminded him that the Tucker and Cordle interests touched at a dozen points; that the Tucker Foundation and the Cordle Trust were associated in a number of charitable, cultural, and scientific projects; that the families had been friends for three generations; that Colly himself had been a guest of the Cordles at Spruce Ledge; that Colly was already in Vermont, not so far from tomorrow's funeral; and that all the other available representatives were busy and Colly wasn't.

"Three p.m.," said Franklyn Tucker. "Get there on time and wear the right clothes."

"Poor guy fell off a mountain," said Colly when he got back to the cabin. "Nobody pushed him. His heart was okay. Seems he just slipped. Poor old Dave. I haven't seen him in a few years but I used to go to their place. House spread all over the hillside like a medieval town, and just as big a population. I liked going there as a kid."

"Then it is right you go to the funeral, *caro*," said Sandro.

"Yes, it is. I'll leave mid-morning and pick up some lunch on the way. Where in hell am I going to get clothes?"

Although the funeral was in a remote place, the attendance was large. All the Cordles staying at Spruce Ledge were there, and the other couples and families in the party. The servants were there, not much noticed in the ordinary course of things, but formidably numerous when assembled in subfusc clothes by the graveside. Gloria and the rest of the summer skeleton staff were there. Many local people were there, farmers, neighbors, shopkeepers from Blue Hill, the Chief of Police and Postmaster and Fire Chief, the schoolteacher and the music teacher and the doctor.

Many people had also come in from far away. Officers of the Cordle Trust and the Cordle companies. Business associates from Wall Street and Park Avenue, and from

21

cities remote from New York, bankers and brokers and corporation lawyers. Very few of them had to come. Almost all could have pleaded distance, or family preoccupations, or pressure of business. They came because they wanted to, or felt bound to. Colly looked round the ranks of white, shocked faces in the Episcopalian church of Blue Hill. A few of the faces were known to him, and many of the names. He sensed real grief. Dave Cordle was truly mourned. These people had *liked* him.

One face mildly surprised Colly: a contemporary of his own, and like himself a one-time Rhodes scholar at Oxford: a man named John Wilkins. John, though from a pretty different background, was not out of place in this company; Colly was surprised only because he knew of no connection. They caught each other's eyes. John made a slight grimace expressive, perhaps, of dislike of funerals and of funeral clothes on a hot day in the country; perhaps of grief and shock.

The coffin was lowered into the raw new grave and the last words were said. A subdued motorcade moved off to Spruce Ledge.

Colly had left his car at the house. He found a place in a Cadillac with some affable elderly Cordles unknown to him; a pink-faced, well-scrubbed husband, a bright-eyed old lady with blue hair.

"Can't understand it," said the husband heavily. "Dave knew every yard of every trail for miles around. Spent a lot of his life here, and spent it on the mountains. How *could* he just fall?"

His wife shushed him. "I don't know what you're suggesting, but I don't want to hear it and Mr. Tucker doesn't want to hear it."

"I'm not suggesting anything. But I still can't understand it."

Colly couldn't understand it either.

The Cadillac threaded the pine trees and rocks to the big gravel apron in front of the house. It was all much as it had been when Colly came as a schoolboy. Memories flooded back. He remembered Dave on the tennis court losing on purpose, in the pool teaching kids to swim, at dinner taking special trouble with a shy young stranger, a girl with glasses or a boy with spots. He remembered him by the stream and on the mountain. He remembered the

22

sure-footed care with which Dave, 20 years older than himself, covered the difficult country. His instructions, what rocks not to trust, what branches not to hang on to. Anybody could slip or stumble. But a fall which could kill must have been down something like a cliff.

The mourners were ushered into the series of connecting rooms, of different heights and sizes, where the Cordles entertained. Voices were low and faces solemn. There was tea; there were drinks.

Colly talked to John Wilkins, a small, serious man with a large head and highbrow tastes. He said: "Why are *you* here?"

"Well," said John, "why are you?"

"Representing the family," said Colly. "Here on my own account too. I used to know Dave well at one time. He was pretty nice to me. But you didn't come here in those days, John?"

"No. But I've been here once or twice this summer. We work for the Cordle companies."

"We?"

"My outfit. Economic research."

"When you say 'my'—"

"Yes, I mean 'my'. I am an economist, whatever I may look like."

"What do you do? Predict the trends in American business in 1984?"

"Yes," said John Wilkins seriously. "Also we do a run-down on a company for anybody who wants to buy it. Or we do an analysis of an industry for anybody who wants to diversify into a new field. Part of what we do is pretty like an investment analyst, part like a banker, part like the U.S. Treasury. Plenty of us in the field, unfortunately."

"Cordle must be a good client to have."

"Yes. That's not the only reason I'm here. Dave pretty well gave us our start. I owe him a hell of a debt."

"So do a lot of people."

"Yes, that's true."

"Well, good luck with it, John."

"Thanks. Good luck to you, Colly."

Colly talked after a while to Fred Bailey, the Chief of Blue Hill's small police force. The Chief was a middle-aged man with a bristling, warlike moustache and mild, peaceable eyes.

The Chief said: "We don't know exactly where he fell *from,* Mr. Tucker. Only where he fell to. We know approximately, but tracks don't show up on dry granite. Does it matter?"

Colly shrugged. He said deprecatingly: "Seems so strange. Dave was brought up here. I never saw him put a foot wrong all the times I walked with him."

"He slipped. Tripped over a branch. Stumbled. He must have. Can you think of any other explanation?"

"Well, I *can,* Chief. So can you."

"Far as we know there was nobody within miles. Doctor says there's nothing in the autopsy to suggest any kind of blackout, loss of balance, dizziness. And he was a guy who had everything. A happy man. Everybody says so and I know it myself. Does that deal with all the possible alternatives?"

"Yes, it does. And nobody has said anything to suggest . . ?"

"No. Well, yes. Why are you asking, Mr. Tucker?"

"I don't know, really. I'm not being ghoulish. Do you mind my asking?"

"I guess not. Well, there's a secretary who says he was worried. Nobody *else* says he was worried. She has a story about a letter. Nobody else saw the letter."

"The mailman?"

"There's a stack of mail here every day. Business stuff as well as personal. There's no trace of any letter came that day that's out of the ordinary. I judge she's taken it very hard. Spinster type. Confidential secretary. They develop an involvement. Transfer all their female instincts to the boss and the job. I don't have any experience of these high-level secretaries, but that's what I understand. Mrs. Cordle says he wasn't worried, not a little bit. He didn't strike me as worried when I saw him only a week before he died. His business associates, I've talked to a few, they say he didn't have any cause in the world to worry. So the view I took, I decided the secretary is overwrought. Her suspicion can be forgotten, in the absence, you see my point, of any evidence at all pointing in the same direction."

Colly had a brief conversation some time later with Camilla Cordle, who was swathed in soft black. She held her head high but her face showed her grief. She did not remember Colly but she knew him by name and asked after members of his family.

He made the conventional noises of condolence which are no easier to make for being genuine. She thanked him gravely.

Camilla said: "I tell myself, 'He shall not grow old as we that are left grow old.' He was not a young man, but he would have hated old age, physical weakness, being dependent. At the same time he did have a life behind him, a long and full and valuable life even if it wasn't finished. It's not like a boy dying before he has the chance to prove himself or do any good."

"There's a lot of consolation in both those thoughts," said Colly.

"And in this one. It seems a terrible, ridiculous waste that he should die in a silly accident, a fall—but he was happy, he wasn't sick, he wasn't the victim of violence. Maybe there was a bad second or two. That's horrible enough. But it's not as horrible as days or weeks of suffering, physical or mental, is it?"

"No, it's not. I think you're absolutely right. He wasn't worried about anything, then?"

"No. Why should he be? I'd know if he was. Even our sons were no worry, which is exceptional enough these days." Camilla smiled slightly.

"I don't want to pry, or upset anybody, or anything, but I heard that his secretary . . ."

"Gloria?" Camilla did not sniff, but she looked as though, if less well-bred, she would have sniffed. "Gloria is a dear soul, loyalty itself, but she's a middle-aged woman besotted by her employer. Not that I blame her. I loved him myself. But in her case it doesn't exactly make for a balanced view of things."

Camilla Cordle and the Chief of Police were talking with the same voice. Colly thought they had been talking to each other about this adoring secretary and her idea that Dave was worried. He thought that the Chief was quoting Camilla rather than Camilla the Chief. He did not doubt that they were both right, but he disliked Camilla's choice of words.

The secretary, it seemed, was called Gloria Baynes. She had been at the funeral service but had now disappeared. "Weeping into a sodden scrap of handkerchief in the office, no doubt," said Camilla, who clearly thought that grief should wear a stoic face, and was the preserve of family and of social equals, which it was presumptuous in a salaried employee to share. Colly disliked her remark even more than the previous one.

A little later, unobtrusively, he asked a maid how to get to the office, which had not existed in the days when he stayed at Spruce Ledge.

He was mildly curious to meet Gloria Baynes, who was said to fit so exactly one of the stock roles of contemporary farce. He was more than mildly irritated by Camilla's attitude to the poor woman. He thought it possible—barely possible—that the secretary was right and the wife and the police wrong.

The offices were an enclave of glossy modernity in the traditional New England territory of the rest of the house. Intercoms, telephones, Telex, files, desks and wall charts were incongruous in a building with patchwork quilts upstairs and hand-made wooden furniture downstairs.

Gloria Baynes was incongruous too. Camilla's snide stuff about "dear soul" and "loyalty itself" had prepared Colly for a homespun figure, a comforting, motherly secretary of the kind apt to darn her boss's socks and bring home-made cookies to the office in an earthenware jar. Gloria Baynes had never made a cookie in her life. She was a city woman, a creature of cool offices and smart bars. Her country stretched from Wall Street in the South to about 75th Street in the North. She was lacquered and case-hardened for survival in that savage jungle. Although she was dressed in expensive, conventional mourning, she looked as out of place in the Vermont mountains as a naked Masai tribesman on Madison Avenue.

Colly shuffled in, unimpressive and deprecating. He said he represented the Tucker family, the Tucker companies, and the Tucker Foundation at the funeral. Of course Miss Baynes already knew this, and had included the information in her handout to the *Blue Hill Republican*. Colly added that he had stayed in the house as a kid, and that Mr. Cordle had been good to him.

"To me too," said Miss Baynes.

"But I guess that doesn't make us special," said Colly. "He was good to everybody."

Gloria Baynes began to cry. Her face wrinkled childishly

and tears spilled out of her eyes. The New York sophisticate gave way to the lovelorn spinster.

Colly considered patting her shoulder. He decided against it. He comforted her with muffled and embarrassed words.

Almost at once she said "I'm sorry." She swiveled her chair so that her back was turned to Colly. She did quick repairs to her face. She swiveled again to face him. She said: "It's ridiculous, but I keep doing it."

Colly said gently: "I don't think there's anything ridiculous in grieving for a person you care about."

"Thank you."

"As a matter of fact, I see something pretty ridiculous in pretending you don't grieve when you do."

"You're supposed to be brave."

"I've known brave people to cry." Colly remembered his beloved Jenny, the bravest person he had ever met, in the brilliant dawn in North Kenya, by the wind-battered oasis of Loiengalani, facing the rising sun with the tears pouring down her cheeks, and cradling in her lap the head of the man she loved, who had been shot through the heart during the night by a Somali poacher. Jenny was not interested in observing any rules except her own, and Jenny was what Colly thought a woman ought to be like.

Colly said: "I can't see any point in wearing a mask among friends."

"But we're perfect strangers, Mr. Tucker."

"I guess devotion to Dave kind of brings us together today, Miss Baynes."

"Yes, I guess it does."

"That's why I can say to you what I don't want to say to anybody else, to any of the family. I simply can't believe that Dave just fell. Not Dave, not here. Not unless he had a heart attack."

"He didn't have any heart attack. And of course he didn't just fall."

"He wasn't pushed."

"Of course not. There was nobody for miles."

"Then he—"

"Jumped. Yes. I think so. That's what my tears are for, Mr. Tucker. Not just Dave's death, but the state he must have been in. I've heard the phrase 'dark night of the soul.' I don't know what it usually means, but to me it means what Dave must have been going through."

"You have, ah, mentioned this idea . . . ?"

"To the police, yes, naturally. I had to. They think I . . . Well, you probably know what they think."

"I don't care what they think about you. I want to know what you think about Dave."

"Does it make any difference? He was alive and is dead."

Colly replied slowly: "I didn't know him as well as you, Miss Baynes, or as recently, and he wasn't as, uh, as large in my life as he was in yours. But I liked and admired him, and he was alive and is dead, and I'd like to know why."

"Then maybe you'll listen to what nobody else will listen to."

"Yes, I will."

"David had a visitor a week before he died. A local man who made an appointment. He sounded funny on the telephone and he looked funny when he came. I wasn't in the room when they talked, but after 20 minutes David told me to get the police here."

"In what terms, Miss Baynes?"

"Pardon me?"

"I mean, did he say 'I have a murderer here in the room', or what?"

"I've racked my brains to remember exactly what he said. It was something like: 'I am holding this man as a criminal.' "

"The crime not specified?"

"No. So I called the police. I brought them in here. The man, Gabetti, had disappeared. I didn't see him go, so he must have gone out through the house. David must have taken him out."

"And Dave said?"

"The man was harmless. He laughed it off. The police were happy to believe him. I didn't believe him. He looked sick. He looked a little bit sick for the rest of his life, for a week."

"What do you believe, Miss Baynes?"

"He must have made a threat. That's when David called the police. By the time the police arrived Gabetti made the threat stick. Then there was the letter. David read the letter and burned it and walked straight out and killed himself."

Gloria Baynes began to cry again.

After a time she said: "Private and confidential."

"How do you know he burned the letter?"

"The ash was in that ashtray."

"Did the police see the ash?"

"No. I emptied it before I went to lunch. I always emptied the ashtrays before I went to lunch. That was before we knew . . ."

"What you're saying is that Gabetti was blackmailing Dave."

"Yes. It's the most puzzling thing of all. I know—I knew—David's whole life, I think. A secretary like me does, its inevitable, it's what we're paid for. All the business side. The reasons for his decisions. His opinions of his partners. Who was getting promotion. What was going well, what wasn't. The personal side too. I bought the gifts. I sent the cables. I made the excuses. I paid the bills. I knew everything he did and most of what he said and a good part of what he thought."

"But not all he felt."

"Not in that last week. No."

"You say you paid the bills."

"Yes. I kept all the checkbooks."

"So you'd know if he made any peculiar, substantial, recent payments."

"Yes I would, and he didn't. The only payments I wouldn't know about would be from the Trust. But that's a charitable foundation. Payments from that are subject to all kinds of controls."

"Everything you say makes your theory more and more difficult to maintain," said Colly diffidently.

"Yes, I know it does. Every few hours I get to telling myself I'm being silly. I even get to agreeing with Camilla about myself. But I come back to all these things. David *couldn't* have fallen. He said Gabetti was a criminal, although he later said he wasn't. He showed him out through the house, which he *never* did to business callers. He burned that letter which he didn't let me see, the day he died. And he looked sick. All that last week he looked sick."

"Sick disgusted? Sick frightened?"

"I don't know, maybe both."

"Fits blackmail."

"But David doesn't!"

29

"No, he doesn't. Have you talked to the Trust people?"

"No. It's all in New York. A call or a letter or a Telex from here, from me, would stir everything up. And they don't have to tell me anything. It's none of my business."

"But payments made by the Trust are no secret? They can't be."

"No, but there's a sort of jealousy. I'm always careful not to tread on any corns."

"Could David make a payment out of the Trust on his own initiative?"

"Yes. A document had to go too. I've typed plenty of them. Because he was acting on his own, he took six times the trouble to make sure the objective was really good. He'd get all kinds of information and put it in the affidavit. He didn't have to. He did it as a courtesy to the other trustees."

"Would the other trustees know about a recent payment?"

"Depends on how recent, I guess. There are two of them here, Mr. Tucker. You could ask."

"I will, Miss Baynes. And then, if it won't distress you, you and I could maybe talk a little more."

Colly went back into the house and to the soft-voiced, sad-faced gathering which was now relaxing into small-talk as highballs replaced teacups. He sought out first one and then the other of the trustees. They were both upright, elderly men, one thin with gold-rimmed glasses, one fat with a pink, polished dome of bald head.

Colly spoke to them both with the voice of the Tucker Foundation. He discussed the agony of choice between competing, equally desirable objects. Administrative difficulties. Necessity for following up donations to see what the money was doing. The hiatus in the summer, when the chance to do something special and imaginative was easy to miss because everybody was away.

"That one we licked, Mr. Tucker," said the fat man. "Dave did quite a bit that was unusual, all on his own. Only the other day he made on our behalf a donation to a group who . . . well, I don't know exactly what they do."

"Doesn't some kind of statement have to accompany a payment made on the authority of an individual?"

"Oh yes. Dave was very meticulous about that. I'm sure there's a full account of the group he gave the money to, everything they're doing and how the money will be spent. But I haven't seen it. I haven't been in New York myself for six weeks. I just heard from the office that the donation had been made."

"When was this, Mr. Cordle?"

"Oh, just the other day. His last act, practically, was a charitable donation. That's representative of Dave's whole life."

The other trustee could tell Colly a little more. The charity concerned young delinquents. It was an imaginative approach. But the trustee had not seen any document written by Dave; he had not been in New York either; he had heard just so much on the telephone.

Colly said that he and other persons involved in the Tucker Foundation were concerned about juvenile delinquency. He was interested in any imaginative approach backed by Dave Cordle. He was referred to the Cordle Trust offices, and warmly invited to make what enquiries he liked.

He went back to Gloria Baynes in the cool, ultramodern office.

He said: "If Dave wrote an affidavit a few days before he died, would you have typed it?"

"Yes, of course."

"Seems he wrote one you didn't type."

"Did he type it himself? I wonder why?"

"Can you think of any reason?"

"He didn't want me to see it. That's the only reason I can think of. But—"

"It's all I can think of too, Miss Baynes. But as you said, these things are not secret. Anybody can look at this document."

"They can, but they wouldn't. If David hadn't . . . if he was still alive and nothing seemed to be wrong, the document would stay on the file and nobody would look at it at all, except the other trustees. And they'd take it at face value."

"We'd better go to New York and see that affidavit, Miss Baynes."

"I can't leave here right now. But I wish you'd look at it."

Colly stood up and shook hands with Gloria Baynes. He

said: "I don't know what we're going to turn up. We may regret starting any of this."

"I realize that. But I think we'd regret much more not starting it."

Colly drove down to the little town. He stopped at police headquarters. The Chief gave him a chair and a bottle of beer.

"What's on your mind, Mr. Tucker?"

"Mr. Cordle and his alleged accident."

"You been talking to Miss Baynes? She's a nice woman and she's smart enough in the normal way, but I'd sooner listen to Mrs. Cordle. What would a secretary know a wife wouldn't?"

"The day you had the false alarm up there. The criminal who wasn't."

"A guy called Antonio Gabetti. There wasn't any complaint filed, but we checked him out. Perfectly respectable business operator, as far as anybody knows. Once upon a time a two-bit hoodlum in Boston, but he went straight years ago."

"Why did Mr. Cordle think he was a criminal?"

"Seems there was a misunderstanding. I guess the English they spoke was a little different. And the man *looks* a criminal."

"Do you honestly think, Chief, Mr. Cordle would get Miss Baynes to drag you all the way up there because a visitor looked like a member of the Mafia?"

"I don't know, Mr. Tucker. And Mr. Cordle is one fellow we can't ask."

"Did you know that Mr. Cordle made a sudden donation to a charity, that day or the next?"

"Typical of the man. Best neighbor this town ever had."

"Couldn't it be something to do with Gabetti's visit?"

"Could it? Like what? Gabetti doesn't run any charity. He doesn't have any money. He says he was trying to sell a big order of pop, they had a misunderstanding, they ironed it out."

"And you believe him?"

"Why not? Confirms what Mr. Cordle himself said. I don't have any evidence pointing any other way."

"Mr. Cordle wrote a document about this sudden donation himself, instead of getting Miss Baynes to type it."

32

"Could be a hundred reasons for that."

"He said Gabetti was a criminal, and had Miss Baynes call you."

"Then he exonerated Gabetti of any criminal intention and said he'd misunderstood the guy."

"He let Gabetti out through the house, instead of by the office entrance."

"Jesus Christ, Mr. Tucker, what are you building on that?"

"Put it all together, Chief, don't you think there's enough to justify an investigation?"

"What of? Who did anything illegal?"

"Of the circumstances of Mr. Cordle's death."

"His death has been fully investigated. I have the Coroner's report right here."

Colly sighed. He thanked Fred Bailey for the beer. He went out into the quiet streets.

The streets of Blue Hill were clean, and shaded by oaks and maples. Sprinklers were playing on the lawns. There were kids on bicycles, and young mothers with baby carriages. Blackmail and suicide seemed impossible in such a place.

Jenny looked up from her whisky as Colly climbed the steps to the rickety porch of the cabin. She said, "Eyes dry yet, darling?"

Colly sat down with a sigh. He picked up Jenny's glass and emptied it. He said: "A very nice lady called Gloria Baynes has reason to think Dave took a jump because he was being blackmailed. I think she may possibly be right. So I have to go to New York."

"All right," said Jenny equably. "Kindly replace my drink before you buzz off again."

Colly looked at the check in the cool, dark offices of the Cordle Trust. "Blue Hill Pilgrims", he read in Dave Cordle's firm handwriting. He turned the check over. The back bore the stamp of the New York branch of a commercial bank in Panama.

"Now why," he said mildly, "would a local Vermont charity use a Panamanian bank? Why not a bank in New York? Why not a bank in Blue Hill?"

The earnest girl who was in charge of the files shrugged.

33

The correct procedures had been followed. It was no concern of hers where people took their banking business.

"Blue Hill Pilgrims," said Colly. "It must be a pretty major outfit to get such a big donation. I wonder why nobody mentioned it at the funeral. I wonder why this group wasn't represented at the funeral. You'd think they'd send somebody along, after a gift like this. I wonder why nobody knew about it."

"Everything we need to know is in Mr. Cordle's affidavit here."

"Yes. Not terribly explicit, is it? Just what's obligatory. I am satisfied that this approach to the problem of juvenile delinquency is imaginative and valid, and that the group constituting the Blue Hill Pilgrims is competent to put our contribution to the best use.' "

"Not explicit? What more do you want, Mr. Tucker? A full dental record of each member of the Pilgrims, with hat sizes and distinguishing scars?"

"I wouldn't mind a name. Just one."

"The trustees will meet these gentlemen in due course."

"Mm. Why do you suppose Mr. Cordle wrote this out in his own hand?"

"Maybe Miss Baynes was sick."

"I happen to know she wasn't"

"Then your guess is as good as mine, Mr. Tucker, but I'd say that under the circumstances *any* guess was a little impertinent."

Colly accepted the rebuke with a bowed, embarrassed head. He went out into the thick heat of Park Avenue.

"Blue Hill Pilgrims?" said Chief of Police Fred Bailey. "No. I never heard of them. Are you sure it's the same Blue Hill, Mr. Tucker? New England is full of places called Blue Hill. Probably Virginia, Kentucky, and a lot of states in the West have towns called Blue Hill. I never went West, but what do you bet there isn't a Blue Hill in Montana? Did you say a bank in Panama? Well, maybe it's a Central American Blue Hill. Maybe it's Jamaica or Trinidad. I guess those places have juvenile delinquency. I'll bet Jamaica has, from what I hear about Jamaica."

"But Gabetti—"

"Who says Gabetti had anything to do with Mr. Cordle's donation?"

34

"The check is dated the day Gabetti visited him. So is the affidavit."

"The same day. I broke the handle off a coffee cup this morning, Mr. Tucker. And the very same afternoon you come to my office. Obviously the two have to be linked, because they happened the same day."

"That's a good point."

"Satisfied, Mr. Tucker?"

"Practically. There's one other thing I want to do. Thanks for your time, Chief."

"You're very welcome. Things are pretty quiet here. They always are."

"He *looks* like a criminal." Antonio Gabetti certainly did.

Colly did not jump to any judgments on this basis. His own appearance was as deceptive as anybody's. His whole *persona*, cultivated with unremitting care over the years, was of an idle, affable, playboy dividing his time between yachts, trout, and the beaches of Southern Europe. Colly knew that many people whose respect he would have liked to enjoy despised him for his life. This was often a pity and sometimes a tragedy. But it was necessary for the job which, partly by choice and partly by accident, was his real life: the job he did in immutable partnership with Sandro Ganzarello and Jenny Norrington, whom together he loved and valued more than all the rest of the world. They all lived lies. They all hid their ruthless, highly-trained professionalism under bushels of self-indulgence. The real Sandro was hidden under a mask of active, even cynical, hedonism; the real Jenny under her veil of marvelous silliness; the real Colly under his laziness.

His was in some ways the most difficult and least sympathetic of their three roles. The European aristocracy had a tradition which made elegant idleness respectable. It was generally known that Sandro's interests were artistic as well as sporting and amatory. It was widely agreed that Jenny's face and figure added visual luster to any party. For them, these things were enough. But Colly's reputation had no such palliative. He was plain lazy, and his laziness was repugnant to his own American tradition. Sententious people might regret the aimlessness of Sandro's life and Jenny's; but nobody despised them. People did despise Colly.

That was the difference. Colly did not think about it often. When he thought about it he sometimes regretted it. Meanwhile he was necessary. The deception must go on. So who was he to judge this repulsive Gabetti on appearances alone?

Gabetti Bottling Inc. was a ramshackle affair, a few sheds at the dusty edge of town. It bottled, and distributed over a small area, a minor brand of pop called Fizzifroot. Some of the sheds had broken windows. There were letters missing from the sign on the roof of the largest shed, so that it read GAB T I B TTLI G NC, and resembled the teeth of a drunkard after a fight. The parking lot was dirty and piled with trash. The machinery of the bottling plant clanked and wheezed. Flies orbited in clouds. No major manufacturer would have dreamed of doing a deal with the firm. It was the bottom end of the American industrial spectrum.

The boss sat under a noisy fan in a cardboard office with flyblown windows. There were three dirty glasses on the desk, and a stack of invoices stirred by wind from the fan. Gabetti was olive-skinned and overweight. He was sharply dressed in the style of the small streets of big cities. Under his arms and across his back his shirt was sodden with perspiration.

He answered Colly: "You know I wenna see Cordle, why ask?"

"He sent for the police while you were there, Mr. Gabetti."

"Sure. He wanted I should give some dough to the police fund."

"Why did he say he was holding a criminal?"

"A gag, I guess. You better ask him."

"Have you ever heard of a charitable group called the Blue Hill Pilgrims?"

"They don't ask guys like me to join a thing like that. I have the wrong kinda name. I came from the wrong parta Boston."

"Were you visiting Mr. Cordle to get a charitable subscription?"

"Naw. I wanted to sell sodapop. Thera's a lotta people up there. I wanted a contract, a weekly delivery. He said no dice. So I left."

CHAPTER THREE

Jenny was sunbathing in a very small bikini near the cabin. There was a tall glass beside her, with a sprig of mint and a lot of ice cubes. Colly lunged for it with a shout. Jenny grabbed it before he got there.

He said faintly: "You can't be so cruel. Not to me."

"Yes I can," said Jenny.

He looked at her with amiable lechery. Her body was marvellous, smooth and slim, looking deceptively soft, pink-gold from the sun.

She caught the look and grinned. The grin made her face asymmetrical, by etching a deep dimple in her left cheek only. Colly's heart lurched as always at this enchanting oddity, which, by being different and unconventional and all her own, was so typical of everything about Jenny. It was all wrong, but it suited her and it was part of her and he loved it.

She grinned, but there was sadness in the grin. She knew how Colly felt about her and always would. For her part she adored him, as she adored Sandro, but the wavelength was different. They all knew all about it, and it was permanent, and there was nothing any of them could do.

Jenny said: "I suppose you've dropped in for three or four minutes. Bloody marvelous host you are. When are you leaving again?"

"Soon as I gargle the taste of Mr. Gabetti out of my mouth."

"You shouldn't eat human flesh, not in this weather."

"A curious guy. He talked like he didn't give a damn whether I suspected him or not."

"What of?"

"Blackmailing Dave Cordle and driving him to suicide."

"Is that what he did?"

"I'm half inclined to think so. I swear he's guilty of *something*."

"Why?"

"What Sandro calls *il mio naso*."

Colly went into the cabin and got himself a long drink. He sat in the shade of the porch, where Sandro lay asleep in a long chair. Colly finished his drink and a cigarette and stood up.

"The yo-yo host," said Jenny. "Up and down. Now you see him, now you don't. You're making me giddy. Why not stay away this time?"

"I just have to go to the can. I mean the telephone."

"All right, if that's what you like. Sandro and I will go fishing."

"No," rumbled a deep voice from the huge and apparently unconscious bulk of the supine Italian in the chair.

"I will go fishing," amended Jenny.

"In all those hot clothes, darling?"

"It's too much, really. I'll take some off."

"Wilkins Research," said a cool voice on the telephone.

Colly asked for John Wilkins, and presently got him. He said: "I'm interested in a company in Blue Hill, Vermont."

"Where you and I were two days ago," said John Wilkins with surprise.

"That's right. I can't get anything out of the company itself. They clammed up completely. And I don't want to stir up curiosity by asking a lot of questions around town."

"What do you want to know about this company, Colly?"

"I don't know until I know it. I mean, I want everything you can find out. Everything. Stuff like how much does the boss pay himself, can the company afford that much, does the way he lives accord with his declared income."

"It's the boss you're interested in?"

"Partly."

38

"We can do a better job for you, more relevant and therefore a hell of a lot cheaper, if you'll tell us exactly what your interest is, Colly. With a completely open brief like this we're going to spend a lot of our time and your money collecting material you don't need. Do you want to buy the company, lend it some dough, put it out of business, start a competitor, or what?"

"For the moment I just want to know about it. You're the only people I know in the business of finding out, so I figured, if you have any spare boys who like New England in July—"

"I have to charge you the usual rates."

"That's understood. I wouldn't have approached you otherwise."

"You can pay a flat fee negotiated now, or cost plus when we see how it goes."

"Cost plus. And I'd like this done tactfully, John."

"They'll never know they're being looked at."

"It's a crummy little job for an outfit like yours," said Colly apologetically. "If you'd sooner not bother with it, give me the name of somebody who'd like the business."

"No no. We'll be glad to take it on. All grist to the mill."

"Mr. Wilkins will be with you in just two seconds, Mr. Tucker," said the girl who showed him in. "Please take a seat. The cigarettes are there."

Colly nodded and grinned. The girl was a good girl. Not morally, perhaps (there was no way of finding out about that without taking more time and more effort than Colly had to spare) but good for some purposes. One of them was showing him into this office and telling him to wait. She did it very well.

Colly sat down. The girl left, returning his grin with a brisk executive baring of the teeth. The two seconds went by, then many more.

It was a pleasant office. It had neither the awesome, stultifying traditionalism of offices under Tucker control, nor the jet-age gadgetry of many modern offices. Nor was it obtrusively styled in any of the conventional modes—pop art, English country house drawing room, colonial Americana, driftwood and *objets trouves*, or action paintings by the Board Chairman's niece. It was like an office. It had maps on the walls. The shelves held reference books. The desk was a desk, not a mountain plateau or a coffee table. The visitors' chairs were chairs, not Madame Recamier sofas or inflated dinghies.

The girl came back into the room with stack of folders. She put them on the desk in a neat pile. She said that Mr. Wilkins was on his way. She went out again. More seconds ticked by.

Bored, Colly stood up and prowled around John Wilkins's office. It was dull. The maps were just maps. The charts were just charts. The books in the shelf were reference books on industry and finance and company law, textbooks on banking procedure and minerology and industrial psychology. The desk was the desk of a busy but tidy man. The out tray was labelled "OUTRE"—a busy, tidy, and sophisticated man.

John Wilkins came in. He apologized for being late and shook hands with Colly. Colly sat down and John Wilkins went round to the other side of his desk. He was a very short man, but when he sat down he grew into a big one. Colly remembered that his legs were the short part of him: his trunk was the normal size. He grew in authority, as well as apparent inches, when he sat down at his desk. He had always been smart, with advanced tastes in music and French poetry, going on from Oxford to the Sorbonne. He was almost bilingual, and, like many musical people, a mathematician. At the same time he was a figure of fun, something of a butt, a complaisant clown. Girls liked him. Maybe he was cuddly. Men liked him too, but they scarcely respected him. They did not respect Colly either, though for different reasons. They *still* didn't respect Colly, but they now respected John Wilkins. This was evident when some of his people came in with the material on Gabetti. Two young men and a frightening girl came in: researchers. They called John "John" but he was most evidently their boss. They most evidently respected him, and Colly did too.

The aides went out, but said that they would all be available if required in the next half hour.

John Wilkins said: "Most of it was pretty easy. A lot of a job like this is simply looking things up in the right books. Desk research. Not all. Now then."

John began to open and look through the material his

aides had left, and the folders the girl had brought in. He said: "Gabetti Bottling Inc. is a sad little company on the edge of bankruptcy. They have a lousy deal with Fizzifroot, but they couldn't get a better one and they couldn't be a concessionaire of a major manufacturer. The plant's in hock. Turnover just about pays bills, salaries, loan-interest, and tax, but it leaves pretty little for Gabetti. Who, believe it or not, has a wife and five kids."

"They eat?"

"Cut-price *pasta*. Now here's the interesting part. Gabetti can just about get by, but he has no money to spare, none for investment or improvement. But he's either just got some or is just about to get some. Quite a lot."

"Oho. How do we know?"

"Because he made deals a few days ago to buy a lot of new bottling machinery and some new Dodge trucks."

"How the hell do you know that?"

"Because we have friends who sell bottling machinery and friends who sell trucks."

"But you don't know where this money is or where it came from or is coming from."

"No. It must be legal, or seem legal. It must be money he really has, or will have. He couldn't afford the interest on another big loan, and he doesn't have the collateral anyway."

"Someone just gave him a present."

"Looks that way."

"Well well well. Three holes in the ground. Tell me more."

John Wilkins told Colly all that there was to be known about Gabetti Bottling Inc. and Antonio Gabetti. It was dull and rather sad. The company was undercapitalized (or had been) and precarious. It was all spelled out from the papers on John's desk: prospects, trading position, local competition, local reputation, standing with the bank, standing in the community. And Gabetti himself had been, even if he no longer was, exactly what he looked: a small-time Boston hoodlum who had done a stretch for stealing from parked automobiles.

"Not one single surprise," John Wilkins finished, "except these contracts."

"And they never knew you were looking?"

41

"Well," said John, "as a matter of fact I'm afraid they did."

"Oh hell, John."

"I'm very sorry. I have, er, reprimanded our man. But under the circumstances he pretty well had to admit."

"What were the circumstances?"

"He was talking to Gabetti's truck-driver, just casually, passing the time of day, in the lot behind the works. Found out quite a few things, incidentally. Gabetti saw him and asked him inside. Obviously smelled a snooper. He went. Gabetti slugged him in the stomach. Then emptied his pockets. Naturally he had business identification. Asked who our client was. Our man refused to say. Gabetti slugged him again. Our boy vomited and nearly passed out. So he said your name."

"I'm sorry he had such a bad time."

"I'm sorry we boobed."

"Gabetti seems to have a guilty conscience."

"It looks that way, but I wouldn't be certain. With back-alley characters like Gabetti it's just instinctive."

"Did your man put the cops on Gabetti?"

"No. He *was* snooping. And it *would* cause a local sensation in a little community like that. We're not privileged in court, like a private detective working for an attorney. Your name would have to come out. In view of your instructions, he figured he'd done enough damage."

"I hope he's okay."

"Sadder but wiser."

"One of the lads I saw?"

"No. He's taking a few days' sick leave."

"I had no idea your business was so tough."

"Nor did he. Nor did I, actually. But we don't investigate a Gabetti every day. And unless you want to get beaten up too, Colly, I should stay away from the place."

Colly was not at once aware of the tail.

He began to suspect the green Chevrolet fastback as his cab churned through the mean tenements of the Upper East Side. He became morally certain as they crossed the Triboro Bridge. He sent his driver a complicated route through Queens, among slab-sided yellow apartment buildings and hole-in-the-wall stores and small grimy factories.

They shook the tail with two quick turns after some

lights. Colly's cab driver was expert but indifferent. A broad Slav face stared at Colly from the driver's identification in the back of the cab. The back of his head had as much expression as his face in the photograph. He answered Colly in bored monosyllables and he drove well and they shook the tail.

Gabetti knew Colly had employed John Wilkins. He would not know for certain why but he would guess. After the interview in which Colly mentioned Dave Cordle he could guess and he would guess right. He might also guess that Wilkins had found out about the contracts for plant and trucks. He might know for certain. He had no way of knowing where Colly was staying in Vermont, so he picked him up at the Wilkins office. Why? To see if he stopped to talk to the police or recruit a private army? To kill him before he passed on his knowledge?

No other tail that Colly could spot picked them up before they got to LaGuardia. The driver of the green Chevy would probably assume Colly was going to J.F.K. Even if he had a two-way radio and called in another tail-car, the other car would be looking for the cab in the wrong place. It seemed likely that Gabetti had kept up his gangland connections; even so he could hardly have mobilized in time a fleet of cars big enough to scour the whole of Queens. He might have LaGuardia watched. It was an obvious precaution. But he could not know where Colly was flying to.

The pilot was waiting with the chartered five-seater Grigg Twin. He was Pete Masters, an old friend of Colly's who had graduated from Air Force jets to a major airline and from there to running his own small company. Colly had financed him and it was a good investment. He still flew a lot. Colly liked and trusted him, and hoped to persuade him to take the time to catch a Vermont trout.

They took off and flew without incident north up the bright line of the Hudson. Idly Colly noticed another light aircraft, far behind and a little above them, flying the same route. They swung east at Albany and the ground began to slope towards the central mountain spine of Vermont. The other aircraft turned also, going to Bennington or Springfield or north of Montpelier. Mount Greylock loomed to starboard, the last sight of Massachusetts. Below was the silver gleam of the Deerfield River. Visibility was perfect and they rode a moderate southwest wind.

The other aircraft remained in sight. Colly wondered about it. It made him uneasy. There was no reason why another aircraft far behind them in the bright air should bother him, but his skin prickled with uneasiness. He pointed it out to Pete Masters, who shrugged.

"Air's getting like Grand Central Station," said Pete. "We already have one-way streets and split-level intersections. Pretty soon they'll need traffic cops and stoplights."

They swung north. Farmland gave way to forest and high scrub and the bald stone tops of big hills.

"Bad place to come down," murmured Colly.

The huge Somerset Reservoir loomed a bright flat blue to the east. Villages nestled in the valleys with their fruit trees and cornfields and sloping pastures with cows and silos. Then the mountains again, not huge but empty and beautiful, no piece of flat ground larger than a tennis court.

There was a small noise from behind, from somewhere aft of the cabin. A little crack, hardly louder than a cap pistol.

"What the hell—?" Colly began.

He saw Pete Masters' face. It was intent, savagely concentrating.

Pete said softly: "She doesn't answer. Nothing from the tail."

Colly said as casually as he could: "Will you go down, Pete?"

"I don't know," said Pete. "We'll go where she goes."

The aircraft began to yaw and wobble in the updraft from the sunbaked granite of the hilltops.

"Buckle up," said Pete. He kept his voice soft. If they were about to crash on the side of a mountain there was no point in shouting.

Colly strapped himself in.

Pete stroked and caressed the controls, groping for a response. The aircraft steadied momentarily.

The ground tilted away as the nose went up. Pete gave her more throttle to avert stall. The ground swung back into sight, but yawned away to starboard as the plane tilted. Trees rushed by under the port side. Pete struggled with the controls, saying nothing, his face intent and angry.

Colly felt angry too. He felt frightened. This was bad

maintenance or sabotage. He did not believe in bad maintenance, not in any aircraft flown by Pete Masters. He was being murdered by a blackmailer. Pete, who had no part in the business, was being sacrificed too. Pete had a wife and two daughters. Colly knew them all and liked them. Pete had nothing to do with Gabetti or Dave Cordle but he was being murdered just the same.

The world swung away from the left and the trees seemed to graze the starboard wingtip. Colly was close to vomiting but he fought with himself because he did not want to die vomiting.

A slab of granite mountainside rushed towards their faces. It came at them very fast as though thrown up at the perspex by an earthquake. The sensation of speed was enormous but time seemed to slow down. Colly had plenty of time to see the blueberry bushes and the stunted pine trees on the broken rock of the mountainside, etched sharply against the grey rock in the brilliant sunshine.

The aircraft threw itself towards the mountainside, but at the last moment the mountain tilted itself away from the nose and rushed by under the wheels. A deep valley, part in shadow, yawned under the starboard portholes. The aircraft lurched and wobbled in the eddying winds of the mountains. The nose dropped and rose and dropped and the horizon swung up and down on both sides.

They lost more height and the aircraft banked steeply over a patch of thick forest at the head of the valley. Colly looked down at treetops terribly close to his right, and up at the clear blue sky to his left. The horizon disappeared in dense green trees.

A wingtip touched a treetop.

Pete shouted something. It was not a word but a wordless shout of anger and despair.

The aircraft slewed in a tight turn. Colly thought it was breaking up. They were flying very slowly. It slapped a tree. There was a noise of tearing and splintering. They bucked violently, boring among the giant treetops. Pete cut the engines. There was a rending, crashing, tearing noise from the aircraft and from the trees. The nose dropped. Colly was still alive. The aircraft had only part of one wing and the fuselage was shredded. The nose dropped and Colly saw the dark floor of the woods coming up at his eyes. There was a noise of rending and splintering. Colly hung in his seat belt as the aircraft ploughed vertically downwards through the branches. This was it. Instinct made Colly contort himself into a ball, head between his knees and arms over his head, in the last split second before they hit. The mutilated aircraft nudged itself downwards through the branches towards the ground.

Gently the floor of the forest came up and hit the nose of the aircraft.

CHAPTER FOUR

Colly groaned. He recovered consciousness. He was hanging downwards from his seat belt. His head ached horribly. He was not certain what he had broken or how much he was mushed up inside.

The aircraft had not exploded. Not yet.

Colly felt confused and battered. He did not know if he could move. He felt unable to make any effort. One clear thought entered the confusion in his brain and dominated it. He must get out of the aircraft and away. He must get Pete Masters out. They must get away before the aircraft blew up. They probably couldn't make it but Colly had to try.

He had a vision of the aircraft exploding. In his vision the intense heat of the exploding gasoline vapor consumed himself and Pete Masters, and then started a forest fire which ravaged the whole of Vermont.

With his right arm Colly clung to the arm of his seat while he tried with his left hand to unbuckle his seat belt. His left hand seemed useless. Colly saw that it was covered with blood. He changed round, trying to grip with his left and unbuckle with his right. He tried to brace himself with his feet under the seat so that he would not fall downwards when he was unbuckled. His right leg had no strength at all, and hurt terribly when he moved it. He thought it was broken.

There was no sound or movement from Pete Masters.

He was in the same position as Colly but the dashboard and controls were all round him. The nose had buckled and Pete seemed to be embedded in the instrument panel. He might be alive.

Colly struggled madly with the buckle of his seat belt with his useless left hand and with his right. He undid the buckle. His legs and left arm were not strong enough to keep him wedged in the tipped-up seat. He fell downwards into the buckled nose of the aircraft. It was not far to fall but it was too far for Colly. He felt a wave of shocking pain from his broken right leg. He passed out again.

He came to. He was half on top of Pete Masters. He wriggled round to the side of Pete's position. It was difficult moving amongst the bent and twisted metal and the shattered perspex. It was difficult moving with one arm useless and with one leg screaming with pain at each movement.

Colly tried to get Pete out of his seat. It was difficult to get at the buckle of the seat belt, jammed between Pete's unconscious body and the broken instrument panel. Pete was heavy and inert. Colly only had one arm that was any good, and every movement hurt his broken leg. The pain of his leg was getting worse rather than better. He was not getting used to it. Colly heard himself crying with the pain. He was continually on the edge of passing out, but he forced himself to stay concious.

He got Pete's belt unbuckled and he started to heave him out of the seat. It was very difficult because of Pete's weight and the awkwardness of his position, and because of the bent and buckled chaos of the nose of the aircraft, and because of Colly's pain and weakness.

Colly dragged Pete inch by inch out of his seat and the tangled ruin of the controls. If Pete had broken bones and internal injuries, Colly was doing them no good by man-handling him like this. But it was better than being burned.

Colly's brain was fogged with nausea, pain, and the enormous physical effort of pulling Pete out of the aircraft. Into the fog of his brain came a trickling noise, the sound of a spilled liquid. Colly did not know if it was gasoline or lubricant or blood. He prayed idiotically that it was hydraulic fluid or water from a battery.

Colly tumbled out of the aircraft dragging Pete with

48

him. Pete landed on top of him on the pine needles. Colly landed half on the raised root of a pine stump. Pete fell across his bad leg. The pain from his back and his left arm and his right leg nearly made him pass out but he stayed conscious.

Colly heard animal noises, wordless agonized grunts. He realized that they were in his voice. He thought he was swearing but he was moaning and grunting like an animal.

The thought of the explosion cleared his brain a little. He pulled his broken leg out from under Pete's body. He heaved himself round so that he could grab Pete round the chest, under the arms, with his right arm. He started to crawl away from the aircraft, dragging Pete as he went. His left arm did not support him, nor his right leg even when he was crawling. He had to crawl a few inches using his good arm and leg, and then use the same arm to drag Pete a few inches.

The ground was rough. It was difficult to drag Pete over it. Pete's clothes caught in roots and rocks, and he was very heavy.

Colly could hardly see. A wet red haze filled his eyes. Pain filled his body. Every inch that he crawled, every inch that he dragged Pete over the steep uneven ground, was timeless agony. He knew that he was going away from the aircraft. That was enough to know. It would not be enough to save them if the aircraft blew up, but it was all he could do.

Crawl. Drag. Crawl. Drag. A few inches at a time. Colly was hardly conscious and he could see almost nothing. He heard himself crying and moaning. He dragged Pete forward. Pete's head seemed to disappear downwards. Colly wondered stupidly where his friend's head had gone. He crawled forward. He put his right hand on the ground. There was no ground. He felt himself falling. He grabbed at Pete to save himself. They tipped over the edge. There was nothing below them.

"Cliff," thought Colly numbly. "Like Dave."

He hung on to Pete. They were not falling but sliding. They slid a long way down smooth rock. Sometimes they rolled. It was a steep slope, broken. Colly banged his head and was knocked out again.

The two bodies rolled together down scree and granite slabs. They went over drifts of dead leaves and pine

49

needles in the hollows, and over low bushes rooted in crannies in the rock.

They came to rest far below in a tangle of bushes.

The aircraft blew up.

The sky was white. There was a crack in it. The crack zigzagged from north to south, then bifurcated into two cracks.

The trees on the mountainside had turned into pink and orange gladioli, which stuck up stiffly near Colly's head. Colly was amazed. But he decided that anything was possible in a world with a cracked white sky.

The woods smelled of ether. A hospital smell. Colly was fully conscious. His headache was gone. There was a dull ache from various parts of his body, but no sharp pain.

Jenny was sitting beside the bed. She was cleaned up. She wore a clean shirt of blue and white checks and she had brushed her hair. The single deep dimple in her left cheek appeared as she smiled at Colly, seeing his eyes open.

She leaned forward and kissed him. He raised his right arm to hug her around the shoulders. His right arm was fine, but he discovered that his left was strapped up. He could think of no reason why this should be, nor did he know why he was in a bed in a hospital with Jenny sitting beside the bed dressed up for hospital visiting.

"What happened?" asked Colly. "Did you throw an ashtray at me?"

"Don't you remember, darling?"

"Nope. Must have been quite a fight."

After a little he remembered flying with Pete Masters from LaGuardia. He remembered the other aircraft behind and above them, and his vague disquiet. He remembered the small percussive noise from behind them, from aft in the fuselage. He remembered Pete struggling with the controls. Nothing after that.

"Pete?" he asked.

"Killed instantly," said Jenny. "I'm very sorry, darling."

"Oh. Oh Christ. Well then, listen. He has a widow called Lydia and two kids—"

"They're here. They came for the funeral. They want to see you."

"They're here now?"

"They're staying in town. Sandro took them out for a picnic today. They'll be along soon, if you're up to it."

"I'm fine. How long have I been here?"

"Two days. You had a bang on the head and that fracture and that other fracture, so they kept you under with jabs of something. Very restful you've been, darling."

"One arm, one leg, one concussion. Nothing else?"

"No. Skull intact. Nothing bust inside. Your guts looked a terrible mess in the X-rays, but they said that was how they were supposed to look."

"Jenny, how lucky I was. I'm terribly sorry about Pete. What actually happened?"

Jenny told him that the plane was seen from a fire-spotter tower to get out of control, bounce among trees, and topple on to the mountain. The fire-spotter was able to get three helicopters up very quickly, which was unusual luck. One saw Colly and Pete and went down to them. They were well away from the wreck. Falling down a steep slope had compounded Colly's fractures but saved his life. When the aircraft exploded he was well clear, and protected from the blast by a spur of hillside.

"I fell down a cliff?" murmured Colly. "Now that's a thing I'd expect to remember."

"Before you did, you dragged Pete Masters about thirty yards. Nobody can understand how you managed it."

"I guess I thought he was still alive. You say the plane went up?"

"Like a torch, apparently. It was lucky the forestry choppers were there. They contained the fire."

"What was wrong with the airplane?"

"We don't know. There's not much of it left. The experts are peering at the bits. They want to talk to you."

"I want to talk to some people too. First Lydia. Then John Wilkins in New York. And a cop called Fred Bailey."

"Take it gently, darling."

"Why? All I have is a bone or two broken. Happens to pro footballers every weekend. Talking doesn't do my leg any harm. Nor does eating, or drinking, or smoking, or . . . I guess some things *do* have to wait."

"So does seeing too many people and talking too much. The crash probably gave your head a wallop. And going down the hillside like Jack and Jill probably gave it several more wallops. They say the X-rays don't show any damage

51

to your great thick skull, but it might have bent a bit. Delayed concussion is an awful nuisance. You pass out suddenly without warning. Awkward if you're driving a car. So go easy, you great fathead."

"That's the true Jenny talking. The ministering angel bit sounded weird. When can I have a drink?"

"In about a year."

"Get out of my room, you limey cow. Do I have to stand for this?"

Lydia Masters and her daughters came in with Sandro. Lydia and the girls kissed Colly. Sandro grinned at him. Sandro and Jenny left the Masters with Colly.

Colly said how much he had liked and trusted Pete. Lydia said it was mutual. In answer to Colly's careful questions she said they were well fixed financially. The Grigg Twin was fully insured and so was Pete, and the other two aircraft and the good will of the business could be sold well.

Colly thought all this was probably true. But he decided he would get in touch with Pete's attorney to find out what Lydia's circumstances really were. He felt horribly responsible for Pete's death. His memory had come back while they talked in its usual full and sharp detail, up to but not including the actual crash on the mountain. He remembered everything that John Wilkins said. He remembered the green Chevy behind his cab. He remembered Antonio Gabetti. It would be very interesting to hear what the scientists made of the bits of the aircraft, if enough survived the holocaust for them to work on.

Colly did not mention any of this to Lydia and the girls. If the aircraft was sabotaged and Pete murdered they would know about it soon enough. Voicing his theories to them now would not help anybody. They knew Pete had lost his life saving Colly's. They knew Colly had risked his life trying to save Pete's. Colly had forgotten that part but they knew about it and they were grateful. It made Colly's life worth saving in their eyes, and this made Pete's death a little less of a waste.

An official from the Federal Aviation Administration wanted to know about the loss of control. Colly told him what had happened.

"A little bang like a percussion cap," the official repeated. "A wire snapping under stress."

"Or what I called it. A bang."

"In my experience, Mr. Tucker, when a man puts a bomb in an aircraft he puts in a big one."

"Then everybody is apt to know about it."

"What we have is consistent with a small explosion. A very limited one. Just enough to stun the controls, simulate a straight breakage. But there's no trace of a device. It's pretty difficult to camouflage a detonator, however small."

"It might have been blown a hell of a long way."

"We searched a long way, Mr. Tucker."

"Is it possible to construct whatever machinery you need out of inflammable material? So you have a completely self-destructive bomb?"

"No. Not in any technology of explosive I ever heard of. There have to be metal parts."

"Could you make it so that all the metal parts looked like something else? Like screws or bolts or bits of springs or stuff, so they duplicated small components already in the aircraft?"

"Whatever the individual parts looked like, assembled they'd give themselves away."

"Sure, but if they blew themselves apart?"

"That sounds a pretty sophisticated toy. Is anybody trying to kill you, Mr. Tucker? Or Peter Masters?"

"I was hoping you'd tell me that," said Colly. "Was it possible for somebody to get near the plane at LaGuardia? I'm not saying somebody got near it, but was it possible?"

"Yes. The place was full of light aircraft and full of people."

"I'm morally certain any plane of Pete's would have been in perfect order. Maintenance and all. The checking procedures. He was terribly meticulous. You probably know all that."

"Yes. We have plenty of evidence that fully confirms what you say."

"Well," said Colly. "It'll be interesting to see if I get rubbed in the next day or two. If I don't, I guess Pete had an accident."

"We prefer conducting our investigations ourselves," said Fred Bailey frostily. "We're not crazy for amateur interference."

"You didn't want to investigate, Chief," said Colly. "Anyway, what I commissioned was business research, conducted by a respectable New York company. They're not private eyes, they're economists. They say Gabetti made these deals to buy a lot of expensive stuff his firm couldn't possibly afford. You know as well as I do he doesn't have any dough either personally or corporately."

The Chief of Police pondered. His manner was still consciously frosty, as Colly had known it would be. His gentle eyes over the ferocious moustache were brooding.

He said at last: "Seems to me you're making two distinct suggestions, Mr. Tucker. One, Mr. Cordle paid a large sum to Gabetti as a result of that visit, maybe masked under this charitable donation you talked about. What if he did? Who knows what his reasons were? It doesn't prove blackmail. It doesn't even *hint* blackmail. How do you blackmail a man like David Cordle? Then, two, you're sort of suggesting Gabetti planted a bomb in that airplane and murdered the pilot aiming to murder you. I understand the pilot was a friend of yours. I'm very sorry he died. Are you telling me Gabetti knew you knew about this money he had, and tried to kill you before you found out any more?"

"I'm doing sums in my head, Chief, that's all. You can do the same sums."

"Sure. Okay. It's pretty far-fetched but in conscience I can't ignore what you're telling me. I'll go lean on Gabetti a little. If that money is real he'll have to explain it. But you know what bothers me?"

"Yes," said Colly. "Finding out what he really had on Dave Cordle."

Fred Bailey nodded. He said: "In police work, or any other line of work, you meet few enough guys who are good all through. You don't want them to fall apart in front of your eyes." He stood up and looked down at Colly in the hospital bed. He said formally: "My best wishes for a speedy recovery, Mr. Tucker."

"Thank you," said Colly.

On the telephone Bailey said: "He spat in my eye. He says he doesn't have any money. He says he didn't make any deal to buy anything. He also has a one-hundred percent alibi for when the bomb, if any, was planted in the airplane. He didn't make any calls to New York, either from his office or from his home. He says we don't have anything on him whatsoever. He's right. So kindly give me the name of the party who gave you the information about those deals Gabetti made."

Colly said: "I'll call them and ask them to get in touch with you."

"Okay. Do it that way round if you think it's more ethical. Only please make it fast."

Colly called John Wilkins.

John Wilkins said: "To tell you the truth, Colly, I don't have any precise idea where my boy got his information. But I'm positive it's sound. He's called Bernard Jones, very bright and very conscientious. If he said Gabetti made a deal, then Gabetti sure as hell made a deal. Very shocked to hear about your crash. Very sorry about the pilot. I understand there are, uh, suspicious circumstances. If so, it could be we bear a burden of responsibility. If the lad hadn't given your name to Gabetti when he was slugged . . ."

"The same lad?"

"Who got the information about the deals? Yes. I think, under all the circumstances, Bernard Jones better get back to Blue Hill and talk to the police personally."

"Well, I think he should. But this is putting you to a lot of trouble and expense, John."

"None of this would have happened if Bernard hadn't given your name to Gabetti."

"He'd better stay away from there."

"I think he'll want to. He still has a sore gut."

"Mr. Bernard Jones," said the nurse.

"Hi," said Colly, surprised. "Lady Jennifer Norrington. Count Ganzarello. Mr. Jones. I thought you were going to Blue Hill."

"I am. I broke the journey to call in."

Bernard Jones was much as Colly had pictured him: a thin, neat, dark-suited young man, slightly but not ostentatiously modern in hairstyle and in collar and necktie. He looked bright but not physically tough. Colly could imagine him adroitly assembling the information about Gabetti's deals to buy machinery and trucks, and getting what he needed out of bankers and civic leaders. He could also imagine him being held and hit by back-street bully-boys, and being terrified by their raw and ugly violence. Looking at Bernard Jones, Colly could not blame him for cracking under Gabetti's threats and knuckle-dusters. Harvard and a good home were no preparation for that. At the same time, his surrender had probably landed Colly here in hospital with a leg and an arm in plaster and two more days in bed; at the same time it had probably killed Pete Masters.

Bernard Jones's manners were very self-deprecating. No doubt this helped him get information from bankers, although it would not help with Gabetti. He seemed, like many clever young men, to have imperfect physical coordination. He blundered about the room in his embarrassment. This was endearing rather than irritating. Jenny smiled at him. All the same, Colly hoped he would not stay too long. Given time, he seemed certain to knock over the flower vase.

Awkwardly he said: "I guess I owe you a very large apology, Mr. Tucker. As far as Mr. Masters is concerned I can't ever wash the slate. What I can do is go on up to Blue Hill and establish that Gabetti did make those deals. That he did have that money, or know he was getting it. I know the money doesn't prove anything, but I guess it's a start."

"Yes," said Colly. "It's a start."

"That's a nice boy, that Jones," said Fred Bailey. "But he got unlucky."

"Did somebody hit him again?" asked Colly.

"I nearly did. He took us over the state line and way the hell down to Pittsfield. We talked to the local Chief and we all went in a bunch to a little office over a barber shop. A machinery broker. Two partners. Respectable little business, and a lot more profitable than it looked. One of the partners died last week. Just died. Nobody shot him. I don't have to tell you, that was the partner who did the deal with Gabetti."

"Nothing on file?"

"It was only at the talk stage."

"But you believe Jones?"

"Yes. He's a nice boy. Sure I believe him. But where does that help?"

"What about the trucks Gabetti ordered?"

56

"We turn around and go all the way into New York state. To Troy. Big G.M. dealer. We talked to the vice-president in charge of sales. A nice fellow. We met all the salesmen. Nice fellows, every one. They had no secrets from us at all. Jones looks along the line of faces. He says: 'Where's Chuck Whoosis? He's the one.' Well, Chuck Whoosis was a motorcycle buff. He'd just taken delivery of a new one, a 500 c.c. Japanese job."

"Don't tell me," said Colly. "He killed himself."

"Two days after Jones talked to him."

"And nothing on file?"

"Do you have to ask?"

Colly said: "How do these coincidences grab you, Chief?"

"Like coincidences. I tried to work it out any other way, any way at all, and it won't go. The machinery broker in Pittsfield had a coronary. He was a Free Methodist, a lay preacher. He was coming out of church, and a gust of wind took his hat. He chased after it. He was 62 years of age and overweight. Make something premeditated out of that."

"Go on."

"The truck salesman in Troy skidded his new bike on a patch of oil. He hit a parked car. He and the bike went right over the car, and the bike landed on top of him. Might not have been fatal, but it was. He wasn't drunk or drugged, and there was nothing wrong with the motorcycle. On the basis of Jones's information we did the routine things. Asked all the questions, and looked at every bit of paper both men had, in the office and at home. Looked through their cars, pockets, everywhere. No trace of a recent deal that even remotely tallies. And nobody saw either man talking to anybody who looks like Gabetti."

"Gabetti might have sent a friend."

"Of course he might. Nobody saw either man talking to a stranger. If they made these deals they both kept completely quiet about them, and made no note of any kind. No memoranda, nothing."

"Where was Gabetti when these people died?"

"Bottling sodapop in Blue Hill."

"Are you sure?"

Fred Bailey was silent.

"Sorry," said Colly. "Please take that question as unsaid.

Where do we go from here, Chief?"

"I don't know where you go, Mr. Tucker, but I quit chasing rainbows and go back to police work."

"No," said Sandro. "This coincidence is not possible. Two men dead who knew Gabetti had money, and one almost dead who suspected him of blackmail. *Una coincidenza cosi meravigliosa non e possibile.* One man can maybe explain it to us."

"Gabetti," said Colly.

"Yes. We must go and ask him."

"I knew it," said Jenny. "You'll want to stay up all night, and I need a lot of sleep. Bangs and crashes. I hate bangs, and I don't like crashes much, either. Go and see him on your own, Sandro. Talk to him as one fat Wop to another. I expect you'll learn much more—"

"You shall come, *tesoro.* It will not be amusing but it is necessary."

"That's right," said Colly smugly. "You go with him, darling. Only leave the Scotch bottle where I can reach it."

Colly had been let out of the hospital. They had come back to the cabin on the trout pond. Until the plaster came off he needed care but not professional nursing. Although it was a short trip, he had insisted on a charter light aircraft for the journey for the sake of his confidence. He had also insisted on one of the Masters' aircraft, for the sake of Lydia's confidence. The aircraft had been covertly but thoroughly guarded before the flight. They had arrived without incident, and Colly had not complained during the jeep-ride to the cabin.

Now it was night and they had eaten the steaks Jenny had grilled, and drunk a small amount of Scotch.

"So we go and see Gabetti," said Jenny, resigned. "What do we do? Torture him?"

"*Si, credo.* He must stop blackmailing people, and I think he must stop killing people. Why do you have that face, *carina?* The first man you ever killed was Italian."

"Yes," said Jenny. "But I've never tortured one."

CHAPTER FIVE

Sandro drove Colly's car. He said he disliked the soft springing and automatic transmission of American cars, but it was a Cadillac and very fast and comfortable. They had a complicated cross-country route to Blue Hill; Jenny held a map and told Sandro where to go.

Jenny said: "He won't be in his office at four o'clock in the morning, fatty. Are we going to his home? Are we going to ask him all those questions in front of his children?"

"We will look very carefully at his office and at everything he has in his safe. When it is morning he will come and we will be there."

"When it's morning a cleaning woman will come. She'll see you, and let out a squawk so loud Gabetti will hear it, and he won't come anywhere near his rotten factory. Or if he comes he'll have a squad of gorillas with 16-inch guns. And all this hurtling about Vermont will be pointless. I ought to be in bed, curled up with a good book."

"With what, *cara?*"

"With my Tarzan comic."

"I do not think signor Gabetti had many cleaning ladies in his office. But if there is one she will maybe answer questions too."

"Are you going to torture the cleaning lady?"

"Maybe. If it is necessary."

They slid into Blue Hill at 3:30 a.m. Colly had told them where to go. They went slowly through the middle of the town. There were no drunks under the big maples of the streets, no nightclubs or discotheques, no banging car doors or noisy farewells. The houses were quietly asleep among well-barbered lawns. A few moths threw themselves at the streetlights.

Sandro drove slowly past the bottling plant. There was a light in the parking lot and one over the door of the office. The buildings were all dark.

"Watchman? Dog? Alarms?" said Jenny.

"Maybe."

Sandro drove on. He turned two corners and parked among other cars in a residential street.

"Bloody hell," said Jenny. "Now we're hiking. Why didn't you drop me?"

Sandro locked the car. He patted his chest and a pocket to make sure he was carrying his gun and cosh and the spool of nylon fishing-line. Experience had taught that the last was often useful. It was clear monofilament, almost invisible in most lights but strong enough to tie up a powerful man, an ideal tripwire, an efficient garotte. They did not often need a garotte but they always carried the spools of nylon. Sandro did not ask if Jenny had everything because he knew that she was armed in the same way and that she would not leave her weapons in the car. It was lucky they had brought them to Vermont. They had not expected to need them, but to be quietly resting and fishing and walking among the mountains. They might have left their pistols behind, in Colly's New York apartment. They had brought them because experience taught that trouble followed them even when they were trying to take a vacation from it: or else they sought it out. This time they were seeking it out because they believed Colly's hunch that a good man had been driven to suicide by a blackmailer, and because the deaths of the machinery broker and the truck salesman were an unlikely coincidence, and because Pete Masters had been killed and Colly nearly killed.

They walked softly back to the bottling plant. Jenny complained bitterly about the length of the walk, but she moved with the silent agility of an animal. She was wearing dark jeans, a black sweat shirt, black sneakers. She had not covered her head; her hair shone like polished metal under the glare of the occasional lights. Sandro wore an expensive Italian version of the same garb. In spite of his great

60

bulk and weight he moved as lightly as Jenny. Nobody saw or heard them on the quiet edge of the small quiet town.

They approached Gabetti's place. They stood in the darkness and inspected it. Its ramshackle squalor was hidden by the warm night. It looked humble and sinless.

A wire-mesh fence surrounded the half-acre of land on which the plant stood. Some of the fence posts had sagged or broken. In places the wire was on the ground. A wheelchair could have gone over it. Colly could have got into the place.

"They're not expecting burglars," murmured Jenny.

The light in the parkling lot illuminated its area pretty well. It revealed a gritty square of asphalt, piles of trash, an empty truck, a derelict car without wheels resting on wooden blocks. Power lines looped in from the street on to big porcelain insulators on a wall.

There was no night watchman and no guard dog.

"Nothing here worth protecting," said Jenny.

"I think nothing."

"Then why are we bothering?"

"We are not here to steal bottles of *aranciata.*"

"Oh no, nor we are. I don't like the sound of Fizzifroot anyway."

Outside in the streets there had been a scent of watered grass and wet soil from all the busy sprinklers of the town which had hissed and freshened from morning until sunset. There had been scents of roses and tobacco plants from the gardens of the houses. Here the smell was of garbage and grease. It was a slum smell, the reek of a different world.

"I don't want to stay here five hours," said Jenny. "I don't want to stay here five minutes."

"*Non e simpatico.* Come along."

The building which housed Gabetti's office was identified by a sign. The light over the door was dim but it made the sign legible. Sandro inspected the door carefully for the wires of a burglar alarm. He did not expect them and he found none. He did not think there would be photoelectric cells or any sophisticated electronics. The door was padlocked, but the metal units which the padlock held could be unscrewed from door and doorjamb from the outside.

"Might as well not have a padlock at all," said Jenny.

"That is right. It is ridiculous. Gabetti does not mind if a thief comes in here. He has no money here, nothing valuable."

"No money? Isn't he supposed to be in business?"

"He does not sell bottles to people who come with dimes in their hands. He sells to bars, soda fountains, resturants. He sends them a bill and they pay with a check to his bank."

"Oh. Then I see less and less why we're bothering with this odious place."

Sandro had removed the screws while they talked. He needed to remove only two. They opened the door and they went into Gabetti's office.

Even in the dark, with only the faint light from outside, it was evidently as seedy as Colly had said. It smelled of dust, spilled beer, and thousands of cheap cigars.

Sandro tried to open a window. It was stuck tight. All the windows were stuck. Gabetti did not like fresh air in his office. The Blue Hill Pilgrims might approve of Nature for delinquent youth, but Gabetti did not want any Nature to invade his place of work. It seemed impossible to open any of the windows without breaking them, but at last Sandro forced one open. He tried to climb through the window, but it did not open far enough for his bulk.

"You must put the screw back, *cara,*" he said.

"What? And lock us in?"

"Yes. Everything must be right when Gabetti comes."

"Suppose he doesn't come till late? Suppose he takes the morning off?"

"Then we have a longer wait."

Jenny sighed. Sandro handed her his screwdriver. She went out of the door and replaced the screws. A close inspection would show that they had been unscrewed and replaced: there would be small, bright scratches in the heads of the screws. Jenny did not think Gabetti would notice the scratches when he arrived in the morning. If he did they might be in a very unpleasant position. They were burglars and he was a man used to violence.

Jenny wetted a fingertip with her tongue. Her fingertip was dirty and tasted bitter. Jenny hoped that not too much rat poison was sprinkled amongst the dust. With her wet fingertip she picked up a little dirt from the asphalt outside the office and smeared it over the screw heads.

She climbed in through the window. Sandro closed the window.

"Oh *no*," said Jenny. "You Wops are all alike. Show you a window and you shut it. Do you like this awful smell?"

"The headlights of a car might just possibly maybe catch the window, make a glare, you know?"

"What a feeble reason. You're frightened of fresh air."

They searched the office for an hour with pencil flashlights. They looked at every paper on Gabetti's desk and in the drawers of the desk. Only one of the drawers was locked. It was a simple lock and Sandro picked it without difficulty. They went through each folder in the metal filing cabinet. Two of the drawers of the filing cabinet held dirty cups and glasses, a half-full quart bottle of rye, some small bottles of 7-UP, and a stack of paper cups. There was also a dirty towel and a tin box holding soap. The soap in the box was strongly scented but the scent was not attractive. Jenny said that she preferred the smell of the stale cigar smoke. The third drawer of the cabinet contained files, and Jenny and Sandro looked at every paper in every folder. They inspected the papers on the floor so that the beams of their flashlights would not be visible through the windows of the office. They felt safe in smoking because of the existing smell of cigar smoke, but they kept their glowing cigarette ends below the level of the windowsills.

All the papers on the top of the desk and in the filing cabinet, and all those in the unlocked drawers of the desk, concerned the business of Gabetti Bottling Inc. They were invoices, receipts, statements, correspondence with Fizzifroot and with customers, bank statements, cleared checks, letters to and from the electricity and water companies, builders, garages, unions, the bank. They were totally consistent with a small, unsuccessful company struggling to make an honest living.

There was no safe in the office. There was no need for a safe.

The locked drawer of the desk contained a stack of pornographic photographs. Jenny inspected them with amazement.

She said: "That bosom can't be real, can it? She's had a transplant from a cow. Two cows."

63

"I think she is real," said Sandro. "But this man? Is he real?"

"Oh yes," said Jenny. "That's nothing. I expect he was a bit cold standing about with nothing on."

Sandro laughed. He put the photographs away. They were careful not to leave obtrusive fingerprints on the glossy pictures. He locked the drawer of the desk.

Jenny sat down in Gabetti's chair behind the desk.

She said: "Now we know everything about Gabetti Bottling. We knew it already."

"Yes."

"And it's nothing."

"No."

"All we've learned is that Colly's chum is accurate."

"Yes."

"What did you expect to find?"

"Nothing."

"But you thought there might be something?"

"I was sure there would be nothing."

"Then what in God's name are we doing here?"

"It was necessary to look. It would have been amateur not to look. We had to satisfy ourselves there was nothing to see. We would have wondered otherwise if there was maybe something to see. Now it is done and we can relax."

"Until Gabetti gets here."

"That is right."

"Or that cleaning woman whose fingernails you're going to pull out. Except no cleaning woman has ever been in here. All right, darling. I'll relax. You can't. We can't both go to sleep, and I'm going to. You'll have to stay awake and watch. Don't call me, I'll call you."

Sandro nodded. He sat in the near darkness by the desk. He sat so that he could watch the door and the windows. He was near enough to Jenny so that he could wake her without using his voice.

Her breathing became slow and regular. She slept in Gabetti's chair. The dim light from outside caught a strand of her hair, but in her dark clothes she was otherwise invisible. Sandro sat and waited for the morning with his gun in his lap.

The dirty squares of the windows began very faintly to lighten. It was as dark as ever inside the office but outside dawn was beginning.

Sandro's mind worked at the questions which the situation asked. He did not find answers that made any sense. He did not understand how an elderly Free Methodist in Pittsfield had been deliberately murdered by a gust of wind which took his hat and caused him to have a coronary. He did not understand how a sober and ambitious young truck salesman in Troy had been deliberately murdered by an oil slick which caused what would normally have been a nonfatal smash. He did not understand how a man who was far away could have done these murders, nor even how his friend who was on the spot could have done them. At the same time, these were the two men who had evidence of Gabetti's sudden wealth. Their simultaneous deaths must be linked. Gabetti must be the link.

The sky was paler. A little daylight was just beginning to filter through the dirty panes into the office. Soon Jenny's hair, and soon afterwards her face, would be visible to anyone who looked in through the windows. It was not likely that anyone would look in, not for hours yet. But it was possible.

Sandro decided to let Jenny sleep for a few minutes longer, before he woke her and made her sit on the floor beside the filing cabinet.

But as he made this decision he saw a movement outside the window which they had opened.

It was possible that something showed, that they had displaced in the dark, without realising it, some large familiar cobweb, or forced through a skin of paint which had bridged the gap between window and frame.

Sandro sat as still as death. If someone was outside it was not a cop making a routine checkup. The movement was too stealthy, there was no sound, there was no powerful beam from a cop's flashlight. It was not a burglary, because any criminal would know that there was nothing here worth breaking and entering for. If it was Gabetti or a friend of Gabetti, how had he been warned?

Sandro thought he was invisible from the window. The window was very dirty. It was still dark inside the office and his hair and clothes were black. His face, although swarthy and unshaven, would show pale, but only very faintly pale until more daylight reached it.

Jenny's hair was another matter. Sandro could just see her face, six feet away. It was dirty from climbing through

65

the window and from the office; it was like that of a camouflaged Marine before an assault. Sandro could see it, but he did not think anyone peeping through the cobwebby and fly-blown window would see it.

But someone outside might see her hair, and every second increased the chance.

Sandro moved only his eyes. He looked hard at the window and at the other windows. He could see nothing. Anybody looking in would be silhouetted against the pale light of the morning. Whoever had looked in, if anyone had looked in, had moved away from the window. The person had either gone right away, or gone to get help, or gone round to the door.

Sandro reached out and gripped Jenny's knee.

She mumbled and awoke. Sandro saw that her eyes were open and that her face was instantly alert. She sat forward in her chair, which made a tiny squeak.

Sandro gestured to the window. Jenny nodded, understanding. Sandro made further gestures, which were a command. Jenny nodded. She slid out of the chair and went to the window which they had opened. She kept low, and moved like the shadow of a monkey. She raised herself very cautiously to look out of the window. She turned to Sandro and shook her head. He gestured again and she nodded. She opened the window. It opened easily now and it was almost silent. She opened it a little way and stared and listened. She opened it a little more.

Sandro heard a key in the padlock of the door. Jenny heard it too. She looked at Sandro questioningly. He nodded. She went like a cat out through the window.

The door opened and a man came in. He switched on the light in the office as he came through the door. He held a fat old-fashioned revolver. From Colly's description Sandro recognized Antonio Gabetti. He was wearing a plaid shirt, sharp fawn slacks, and sloppy loafers. He was unshaven and his hair was unbrushed. He looked wide-awake and mean. He had just got out of bed and hurried here, with his gun, and come into his office expecting trouble. Why?

Sandro did not move. Gabetti gestured upwards with his gun. Sandro raised his hands.

Jenny came in behind Gabetti.

She said. "Drop it, Mr. Gabetti, or I'll shoot your backside off."

Gabetti lowered his gun but did not drop it. Jenny hit him with her gun-barrel hard on the wrist. He grunted and dropped the gun.

Sandro picked up his own gun from his lap. He stood up. He said politely: *"Accomodiamoci, signore."*

Gabetti looked at him searchingly, his black pig-eyes narrowed with resentment and suspicion. He sat down in the chair Sandro had vacated.

Jenny took out a handkerchief. With it she picked up Gabetti's gun and put it on top of the filing cabinet.

Gabetti said: "Who the hell are you? What is this?"

Sandro said: "Before we talk I will say two things. First, my friend and I have killed many people and we do not mind killing you. Is that quite clear? Second, if any of your staff come in, or anybody else, we are peacefully here on business. We are selling insurance. If you remember that you may stay alive. If you forget it you will certainly be shot and perhaps the other person also, if I decide. You understand?"

Gabetti showed that he understood.

Sandro said: *"Carina,* tie his legs to the chair so that the line is hidden under those ugly yellow pants he wears."

"Hey," said Gabetti.

"If he gives trouble, knock out some of his teeth with your gun."

Jenny produced her own nylon fishing line from the hip-pocket of her jeans. She lashed Gabetti's legs just above each ankle to the legs of the chair. His legs were thick and white and the fine nylon bit into them. Jenny had some compunction about hurting Gabetti but not much. She pulled the cuffs of his trousesrs down over the lashings to hide them. She did not like touching Gabetti or his clothes.

Sandro said: "Why did you come here at this time of the day, suddenly from your bed?"

"Saw da Caddy, waitin' outsida my house."

Jenny laughed.

Gabetti said: "A guy came saw me a few days back. He had lotsa questions. I remembered his car an' parta da number." In fright and stress his English thickened and deteriorated. He was more than ever the archetype of the cheap Italian hoodlum.

"An amusing chance," said Sandro, "that I chose your house to park. *Molto comodo*. Okay. I am a friend of that man and I too have many questions. But I ask in a different way. He is polite and kind, but I ask my questions with a gun and a cigarette-lighter, with a knife and this pair of pliers and plenty of nylon rope, and with other things to make you beg me to kill you if I use them."

Jenny knew that Sandro was putting on an act, but he looked and sounded extremely grim. He looked more than ever enormous in the cramped office, with the single harsh unshaded bulb hanging above his head. Jenny thought Gabetti would believe Sandro's threats and would be very frightened of him.

"Cheez," said Gabetti. There was no defiance in his voice.

He talked at once.

He said that a man had come to him with a proposition. It was worth $50,000.

"Describe the man."

Gabetti tried, with fear in his voice and sweat running down the yellow folds of his face and into the heavy stubble on his cheeks. But his vocabulary was small and he was not good at description. He was no good in Italian either. He said the man was around thirty, around five-ten, around one-sixty. He wore ordinary clothes, a tan suit. His face was normal, a white man, not a spic or a dinge, not a sheeny, not a person of Italian blood. His appearance had not interested Gabetti but his proposition had.

Gabetti was to make an appointment with David Cordle at Spruce Ledge. He had never met Mr. Cordle nor been to Spruce Ledge, but of course had heard of the local millionaire. Everybody in Blue Hill knew about the Cordles and their summer palace in the mountains. He was to see Cordle alone and to ask him for $100,000 for a charity. The name and function of the charity were given to Gabetti. He was rehearsed in what he should say about the charity.

He was given information about Cordle which he did not believe. He was shown photographs and then he did believe the information. The photographs were of Cordle and another man in a small bare room. They were dressed as little girls while they were still dressed. There were a lot of pictures, in sequence like a movie. Gabetti described,

68

uncouthly and obscenely, what the pictures showed. There were also tapes, but Gabetti did not get to hear the tapes. Gabetti told Cordle about the pictures and tapes, and about the list of people both were to be sent to.

"So Cordle gave you a check?"

"He sent it. I passed it on."

"Where?"

"Here. To the same guy."

"Where is your half?"

"I didn't get it yet."

Sandro said: "Okay. In some minutes we ask that question again. First you will tell me what happened to the airplane."

Gabetti said he did not know what happened to any airplane. He became very frightened of Sandro but he persisted that he did not know about the airplane. He did not know about a dead machinery broker in Pittsfield or any truck salesman in Troy. He said he had never been to Troy. He had not been to Pittsfield in three years. He had not made any deals to buy machinery or trucks.

"You are lying," said Sandro gently.

"I swear, lissen, ya gotta believe me—"

"He is lying," said a voice from the open window.

Immediately there was a thud, not loud, from the window. An extra eye opened above Gabetti's right eye. He slumped sideways in his chair.

CHAPTER SIX

The silenced pistol thudded a second time and a third. The second round clipped the edge of the desk, behind which Sandro had dived. The third hit the slumped corpse of Gabetti in the shoulder. It slapped into the dead flesh with the noise of a hand slapping the flank of a horse. Jenny was behind the chair which held the body.

Sandro had not immediately known whether to fire at the killer. A man who killed Gabetti was by no means necessarily an enemy in this confused situation. He might be a friend of David Cordle. But now he was firing at them and the question was answered. Sandro took a snap shot at the open window, from the floor level and round the corner of the desk. At almost the same moment he heard Jenny's gun. But the silhouette in the window had disappeared.

Sandro ran to the door of the office and turned off the light. There was no point in making it easier for the killer. He went to the window and looked out carefully. It was almost full daylight but the world was still asleep. There was no one to be seen in the squalid parking lot. But there was a lot of cover, from the other buildings and the truck and the derelict car and the garbage cans and piles of crates.

Sandro postponed speculating about the killer. A lot of questions must be asked but they must wait. The thing now was to get out of here without being shot. It would be a good thing also to shoot the new arrival. He had tried to kill them, presumably because Gabetti was talking. He would try again. They were both easily recognized. Jenny could be disguised but there had never been any way of disguising Sandro. Perhaps they could be linked to Colly, and Colly was helpless with a broken arm and leg.

Sandro did not trust the flimsy wall of the office. The killer's gun was not a heavy weapon; it was small enough to carry a silencer. But he might not be far away and his bullets might go through the walls of the office. Sandro needed a shield. He heaved the filing cabinet to the door, and stood it beside the doorpost on the side away from the hinges. He gestured to Jenny to stay in cover. Keeping the filing cabinet in front of him he reached to the door handle and pulled the door open.

As he expected there was an immediate response. The silenced gun thudded. It was a good shot. The bullet hit the side of the filing cabinet. If the cabinet had not been there it would have hit Sandro. It ricocheted at one of the dirty windows and exploded the glass outwards into the parking lot.

The shot came from behind the truck. The truck was parked near the door of the main bottling shed. It was ready to be loaded with crates of sodapop. The killer was behind the cab of the truck. No part of him was visible. He was in a good position. He could get away when he liked. Meanwhile he commanded the office building and most of the parking lot. Sandro was safe from him, but he could not go out of the door of the office. He was only safe while he stayed where he was. There was no point in firing at the truck. He had to expose himself to shoot, he had to shoot left-handed, and his gun was not silenced.

At the same time, although the killer could get away he could not harm Sandro. Evidently he wished to kill Sandro and Jenny, not merely to get away after killing Gabetti.

It was stalemate, and every moment the daylight strengthened and brought nearer the time when the place would be full of Gabetti's workmen and the quiet street of people going to work.

Neither Sandro nor the killer could move so as to threaten the other, but maybe Jenny could move. The open window was not visible from the truck.

Sandro said softly: "Maybe you can take him in the rear."

71

"There you go again," said Jenny. "Whenever there's an errand I have to run it."

She slid across the floor and once again out of the window.

Jenny landed on all fours on the dirty asphalt. The daylight cruelly exposed the impoverished squalor of Gabetti's premises. It was a depressing place to have a fight and Jenny was aware of being very dirty. She saw that her hands were filthy and she guessed that her face was filthy too. This would not normally have bothered her, but she thought it was unseemly to be shot when she was looking so disreputable. She devoted herself to the problem of getting to the other side of the truck without being shot.

She was near the perimeter of Gabetti's property. There were no buildings to give her any cover. The wire mesh fence had sagged to within inches of the ground in some places. There were patches of milkweed and coarse grass along the line of the fence, but they were not continuous cover and they were not very good cover at best. Behind stretched a waste and sandy area of several acres.

Jenny backed away from the office, keeping the dingy little building between herself and the truck. She crossed the perimeter fence and considered the position. She disliked it very much. She had to go fifty yards before she was in the protection of another building, and before she could get at the man behind the truck. She could take a very big detour round, so that she was out of range of the killer's pistol. But then he would be out of range of her pistol, and she could give Sandro no help if he needed it. He might be struck by a splinter; the killer might throw a petrol-bomb; there were many possibilities. She must stay within call and the killer must be within range of her gun.

It was therefore a choice between crawling and running. Crawling would take a long time. It was not safe. There were stretches with very little concealment, where the grass and weeds were thin and the fence flat to the ground. Jenny was revolted by the thought of a fifty-yard crawl in bad cover.

The man was a good shot. He had hit Gabetti an inch from his eye. He had very nearly hit Sandro at twenty yards when the target was small and moving fast. But to hit someone running, at twenty yards, with a pistol no bigger than a .32, would be very difficult and lucky. Jenny did not want to run fifty yards in the open but she decided it was the best thing to do.

She ran.

She half-heard two or three thuds from the truck, and once the crack of Sandro's bigger .38.

She was not far from the cover of a shed when her foot caught a trailing bramble and she fell headlong. It was a hard fall because she was running as fast as she could. The ground was hard and she fell heavily and painfully. All the breath seemed to be knocked out of her body and for a moment she was half-stunned. She did not hear another thud from the gun but she heard a bullet whack into the ground near her head. She fired once, wildly, in the direction of the truck, and then scrambled to her feet and ran into the shelter of the shed.

Her breath rasped painfully in her lungs and her face was bleeding from hitting the rough dry ground. There seemed to be no skin on her knees or arms or knuckles. Her breast hurt and her hand was shaking. But she had not been shot and she was in cover.

She gave herself a necessary moment to get steady. Then she dropped to ground level and peeped round the corner of the shed. The truck was head-on to her. There was no one in the cab or behind the truck. The door of the main bottling shed was ajar. Jenny thought it had been shut. She thought the killer had gone into the bottling shed.

The shed was the biggest of the buildings, the one with the gap-toothed lettering along the top. It was partly brick-built, with a corrugated asbestos roof and high windows. The windows were too high to see through for a man on the ground. The killer would not climb up inside to see out of the windows because he would then be terribly vulnerable to anyone who came in. Was there another door?

Jenny stood up and gestured to Sandro, who was hidden from her in the open door of the office. She covered the door of the bottling shed as Sandro came out of the office. He ran to the truck and covered the door of the shed.

Jenny said: "I'll see if there's another door."

"Okay, *cara*."

Jenny ran to the bottling shed and went carefully round it. She did not want to be ambushed at a corner. There was another door in the far end of the shed. It was a large double-door of galvanized metal, padlocked on the outside.

73

It could not be opened with a screwdriver like the door of the office. It could not be opened from the inside. It was the only other door. The gunman was trapped inside the shed, but he had wonderful cover and perhaps local knowledge. It was impossible to go in after him.

"Now what?" said Jenny.

"First untie Gabetti's feet."

"Ugh."

"Then telephone the police. Say like this: we made an appointment to talk to Signor Gabetti, we met him here, we had a peaceful conversation, he was shot through the window by a man who tried also to shoot us. We have no guns, but we have Gabetti's gun."

"Oh yes. How lucky he brought one."

"Explain where he is hiding and suggest they bring some tear-gas."

Jenny nodded. She trotted to the office and cut the nylon. The fine line left marks on the ankles of the corpse which would immediately be spotted by the police, but there was nothing to be done about them. She put the nylon line in a drawer of the filing cabinet. There was no need to make it instantly evident that they had tied Gabetti to the chair. She pocketed Gabetti's gun.

She picked up the telephone. It was dead. She went out of the office and found where the line went through the wall by one of the windows. The line was cut close to the wall. The gunman had cut it before he shot Gabetti. Jenny could think of no reason for this. It was annoying.

Sandro said: "Then you must go to the car and fetch some policemen."

He glanced at her, taking his eyes from the door of the shed for a fraction of a second. What he saw changed his mind. He said: "No. You watch this door and I will fetch the policemen."

"Why?"

"Because you look terrible. You have run away from reform school. You have been in six fights with drunk sailors you tried to rob. You are not respectable. The first policeman who sees you will put you in his jail as a vagrant."

"Oh. Yes. All right. What snobs these New Englanders must be."

"Give me your gun and anything else you have."

74

Jenny agreed reluctantly. She gave Sandro her gun and cosh. He would stow them, and his own weapons, in a part of Colly's car where they would not be found. Jenny hefted Gabetti's enormous Colt, a larger hand-gun than she had ever used.

She said: "I agree we need a bit of help. But wouldn't it be nice to wait till the staff come? Then we can sit on top of this mousehold together."

"I thought of it, *cara*, but no. The staff may be like Gabetti. I do not want them to find Gabetti, and us, before the police are here."

"I see what you mean. I expect you're right."

Sandro pocketed Jenny's gun and his own. He did not tell her to be very careful because he knew it was unnecessary. He did not say that he would be as quick as possible because he knew she already knew this. He turned to go.

A gun cracked from the derelict car. Sandro grunted and clutched his thigh and slowly collapsed towards the ground. Jenny fired at the windscreen of the car. She held the heavy old pistol in both hands but it jumped as she fired. She fired again. The bang was very loud and the pistol kicked like a mule. The windscreen of the car exploded and a man fell sideways out of the car. His face was a mask of blood from the shattered windscreen. He looked dead.

"That's enough," said a voice sharply from the open door of the bottling shed.

Jenny froze. Despair filled her. There were two of them. One had been hiding all along in the derelict car, waiting for just this moment. He had got unlucky, but they were unlucky too. Sandro was hit and the other had the drop on her. This other had killed Gabetti. Jenny supposed he would now kill her. But she did not want to turn probability into certainty by trying to spin and get off a shot. Probably he was invisible to her in the doorway, and he was a very good shot, fast and accurate.

She dropped the Colt and turned. She could see the long tube of the silencer of his gun in the doorway. It was pointed at her. There was nothing else to see.

Sandro groaned. He was conscious and armed. There was hope.

The voice in the door said: "Take the two guns out of

your friend's pockets and throw them a long way away. If you do anything I don't like I'll shoot you in the kneecap."

The hope which had briefly flared in Jenny guttered and died. She felt a greater despair for the moment of hope.

She bent over Sandro. He had passed out. She took his gun and her own and threw them towards the derelict car. The man who had fallen out of the car had not moved. He was a terrible sight. Jenny realized she had shot him full in the face and bullet and glass together had removed his face. She felt ill.

She straightened and turned again toward the door of the shed. She did not understand why the gunman did not shoot her at once with his safely-silenced gun, and then finish Sandro off.

"Be my guest," said the voice behind the silencer.

Jenny walked slowly to the door. The pistol disappeared. She followed it into the shed. She supposed she would be asked questions before she was killed.

She glanced round the bottling shed. It was about fifty feet long, a bolted metal-frame structure with rough brick walls to six feet and then wooden planking. The long windows were ten feet from the ground.

The far end of the shed was stacked with thousands of empty bottles on big trays. They had no labels. They had been brought in from being washed in another shed. The end near the door was stacked with full bottles in crates. The crates were waiting to be loaded on to the truck. In between was the primitive production-line of the plant: a belt which carried the bottles through various machines and emitted them full, capped, and labelled. A regiment of empty bottles was waiting ready at the far end of the belt so that bottling would begin the moment the machinery was started.

Each machine seemed to have controls, but Jenny imagined that the line was automated. A single master-switch would start all the machines simultaneously with the belt. She saw what looked like a control panel not far away on the brick wall. Heavy power lines came through the wall and down by insulators to the panel.

The killer was standing by the wall, well away from the belt, fifteen feet from the door and from Jenny. He was in shadow and it was difficult to see him clearly. He looked very ordinary. Jenny remembered Gabetti's words—thirty, five-ten, one-sixty, normal clothes, normal face. What Jenny had heard of his voice was normal too. Not obviously ill-educated like Gabetti's, not pedantic; not Bostonian or Deep South or Brooklyn.

He said: "Start talking. Your friend can have medical attention as soon as I have the information I want."

Jenny said wearily: "What do you want to know?"

"You British?"

"Yes."

"Remember Bunker Hill. All right, England. Why did you and your friend come visit Gabetti in the middle of the night?"

Jenny thought she must tell as much of the truth as possible because this man had heard Gabetti talking. But she must not tell enough of the truth to implicate Colly. She did not believe Sandro would get medical attention, but a bullet: but they might not read the link back to Colly, whoever they were.

She said: "My friend was a friend of David Cordle."

"So?"

"He said Mr. Cordle wouldn't have fallen off a mountain. He committed suicide because he was being blackmailed."

"Who by?"

"He wasn't sure but he thought Gabetti."

"For what?"

"Gabetti said $100,000."

"I mean, what guilty secret did Cordle have?"

"He liked dressing up and having his bottom smacked."

This was easy so far. Jenny covered familiar ground with her answers, leaving part of her brain free to make plans. She had no real thought of getting out of this but it was silly not to try. She remembered other disagreeable situations. Shot full of dope and a prisoner on the yacht of the Man with the Tiny Head. Alone with a sadistic Amazon—her particular enemy among the abominable Priests—on an island in a Highland loch. In the path of a herd of stampeding elephant in the North Kenya bush, the animals maddened by the drug-tipped darts of ALA. And held in the silent attics of an Amsterdam brothel by the green-clad armies of Intergard. This was no better than any of those but it was no worse. She had got out of them. But of course she had had friends beside her, Colly and Sandro fit and mobile. Now she was alone in a seedy little factory in a strange country, alone with a professional killer who thought she knew more than she should.

"I see," said the killer. "How did Gabetti know?"

"A stranger told him."

"How did the stranger know."

"Gabetti didn't say. I don't think he knew."

"Try again."

"Perhaps Gabetti did know. He still didn't say."

Jenny had allowed her shoulders to sag in evident despair and dejection. She slightly bent her knees. She lost an inch or two in height by standing, sacklike, in a posture of defeat.

The man said: "Have you talked to the police about this?"

"Yes, of course."

"Do they know Cordle was a sexual deviant?"

"I don't think so. We only heard that today from Gabetti."

"I see."

Jenny jumped. Because her knees were already bent she was able to jump without a preliminary crouch. Her lackadaisical attitude had made her look incapable of sudden movement. The gun was still pointed at her but she thought the killer would be taken by surprise. It would not traverse quickly and she thought she had a chance of being quicker. She jumped low, diving; she dived behind the last of the machines.

The gun thudded. The bullet smashed into the ranks of full bottles of sodapop. There was a great explosion of fizzy pop. Glass showered over Jenny and the machine and there was a sick, sweet smell of fruit.

Jenny grabbed a full unbroken bottle and hurled it at the gunman. It missed him and crashed into the brick wall of the shed beside his head.

The gun thudded again. There was another explosion of sweet, fruity pop and another shower of sticky fluid and of glass.

Jenny tried to remember how many times the man had fired and how many rounds there would still be in his magazine. She thought he could not have more than three rounds left. But he might have a full spare magazine.

Jenny dived again. She dived to the control panel. The

78

gun thudded again as she dived. The bullet ricocheted off a flange of metal by the conveyor belt and whined dangerously round the shed.

Jenny began throwing switches on the control panel: any switches, all the switches. None had any effect at all. None started a machine or even turned on a light. She wondered, in a flash of renewed despair, if the killer had cut the power lines as he had cut the telephone line, or if there was a master switch somewhere else that had to be operated first.

The killer advanced delicately towards the belt. He leaned the silencer on his free arm like a target marksman.

Jenny threw a last switch, the very last of the switches on the control panel.

There was immediately a noise like thunder and everything began to shake and rumble. The belt lurched forward on its interminable journey. The empty bottles at the far end of the belt jiggled into motion like a rank of drunken soldiers. They clanked to the first machine which squirted an inch of bright colored essence into each. They clanked on to the second machine, which filled each bottle very quickly to the top with carbonated water. Full and bubbling, they jiggled on to the third machine.

The gunman was beside the third machine. Jenny could still not see his face clearly. It looked calm and business-like, neither gleeful nor sorrowing, not at all upset by killing or by the noise of the machinery or the sickly, overwhelming smell of the fruit essence.

Jenny ran. She ran to the far end of the shed. All she could hope for was that the killer would be distracted by the noise and movement and would shoot wildly: and that he had very few rounds left and no spare magazine. She ran to the far end of the shed, dodging. She tripped over a cable. She fell as she had fallen outside but it was more painful. The concrete floor was harder than the ground and she was already bruised and cut by the first fall. She hurt her knee and elbow badly when she fell and she was winded.

The gunman leaned over the moving belt to get a shot at Jenny at his leisure. She was helpless on the ground and it was time to kill her. He had some clearing up to do before he left, and the staff would arrive in an hour. The bottles advanced up the belt. His coat trailed over the belt as he aimed. The advancing bottles picked up the skirt of his coat. They clanked on into the machine which slapped metal stoppers on to the bottles and squeezed them tight. They pulled the coat into the machine. A stopper went on to the first bottle, thrust down by a piston from above. It caught the hem of the coat. The coat was pulled into the machine. The gunman fired, but he was pulled off-balance by the machine and the bullet went far up into the wood above the brickwork. The gunman struggled to get out of his coat or to pull his coat away from the machine but he did not have time. The piston clamped down on to his hand with a metal bottle-top. He screamed. The machine pulled his hand inwards and the piston clamped a metal bottle-top on to his wrist.

The machine was indifferent to the screams of the gunman. The piston was indifferent to a softer landing-place than the glass lip of a bottle. The sharp serrated edges of the bottle-tops were indifferent. The machine did not mind a shorter distance for the piston to travel because it was used to different sizes of bottles and adjusted itself automatically. The gunman's arm and shoulders were pulled into the machine and the pistol stamped bottle-tops down on to them.

Jenny came to. She struggled painfully to her feet, amazed to find herself alive. She staggered to the control panel and turned the machinery off. A huge silence fell. The gunman in the guts of the machine was a terrible sight. Everywhere there was broken glass and sticky spilled sodapop.

Jenny walked to the door of the shed. Her feet crunched on broken glass. She felt tired. She went out into the flat early morning light. It was not yet sunrise. Very little time had in truth passed since the extra eye had opened in Gabetti's yellow face.

Sandro was conscious. He had picked up Gabetti's gun, which was nearest, and had crawled almost to the door of the shed. His face was grey with pain but he said: *"Ciao, carissima. Come stai?"*

Jenny went down on her knees and kissed him. He embraced her. She cut away the trouser-leg over his wound. She thought the bullet had hit neither artery nor bone, but it must have carried in some of the fabric of the trousers and it needed attention fast.

She said: "The quickest doctor will be the police."

"I think. Get the car. Hide our guns. Gabetti killed that man with no face, yes? With his gun. I think so."

Jenny went to get the car.

CHAPTER SEVEN

"Pictures and tapes?" said Chief of Police Fred Bailey. "Picture and tapes of what?"

"We don't know," said Jenny.

"How did Gabetti get anything like that?"

"I don't think he did. He was just a messenger."

"Why would this stranger use Gabetti? Why wouldn't he go to Mr. Cordle himself?"

"We don't know," said Jenny.

"What you're telling me is that the fellow who fell into the machine, and his pal who accidentally shot the count here, found out something, something about Mr. Cordle. They used Gabetti as a go-between. Gabetti got in touch with you because you were friends of Mr. Tucker. He started to tell you all about it because he hadn't been given his cut and he was sore, but he was scared to come to us. Then the other two happened by the place, and Gabetti shot one of them and the other one shot him. I never heard anything so screwy in my life, Lady Jennifer, frankly."

"Why? They shot each other because of the money, don't you think?"

"I guess so. That's the only part that makes sense. I'm glad I never learned what they had on Mr. Cordle, if any of that was true. But it's a very messy and inconclusive business."

"Certainly messy," said Jenny, remembering the machine which stamped the tops on the bottles.

"How did Gabetti get those marks on his ankles?"

"I suppose we'll never know, Chief."

"You'll have to give evidence at the inquest."

"Yes."

"You'll be on oath."

"Yes."

"Things like this," said Fred Bailey gloomily, "don't happen in Blue Hill."

Sandro's wound was dirty but the bullet had missed the bone and blood-vessels. He was given antibiotics and a sedative. It was painful and he could not walk. The police surgeon found him crutches which he promised to return.

They promised to keep the Blue Hill police informed about their movements. The police promised to keep their address secret.

Jenny drove the Cadillac out of Blue Hill. She got away ahead of the reporters. She went a circuitous back way. On a stretch of empty backroad between farms she stopped and unpacked their guns. She waited for a few minutes by the car, listening. There was no other car. They were not being followed. They were disappearing into the mountains. This was necessary in case the killer and his friend had other friends.

"I'll tell you what I don't believe," said Jenny.

"What is that, *cara?*"

"$100,000. It's too small. Cordle was a multi-millionaire."

"The figure is right. Colly saw the check in New York."

"I know it's stupid, but it's wrong all the same. If Gabetti was getting half, those two were only getting $25,000 each."

"That was the first bite. There was the letter, yes? The letter the secretary said he burned, the day that he died. Maybe that was the second bite."

"Yes, but if they were doing it by letter, why bother with Gabetti at all?"

"Why? There is much I do not understand."

"Me too, and I'm not even going to try."

The dead man in the machine was wearing moderately expensive clothes. His suit and shoes had been bought in Schenectady. He had no driver's license or credit cards. His billfold, which was old, held only $43 in cash, a few postage stamps, and the business card of a General Motors dealer in Troy. His only identification was a letter addressed to Wayne Redmond in care of the All Seasons Motor Lodge, Blue Hill. He tallied with the description of the stranger given to Sandro by Gabetti, but so did half the thirty-year-old male population of New England and New York State.

The other man was smaller and a few years older. His face was impossible to reconstruct. He had extensive dental work, not new. His clothes were all from a famous store in Boston. He carried no identification at all.

The manager and a maid at the hotel recognized the men, the second by his clothes. They had checked in two days earlier. They shared a cabin. The register said they were Wayne Redmond of Schenectady and J. R. Purvis of Boston. Both signatures looked educated. They arrived in a car with a third man who drove the car away. Nobody could describe the third man. The car was a new tan Chrysler with Vermont plates. It did not belong to anybody in Blue Hill. Nobody could remember the number. The same car, or its twin, returned to collect both men an hour after they arrived. Each carried a small case. The manager was surprised by the cases. He checked the cabin. The rest of their luggage was in the cabin. The men were not seen to come back to the motel, so it must have been late at night. They made themselves instant coffee in the morning. Sachets of coffee and of powdered milk, and an electric kettle, were provided in each cabin by the motel. The maid washed up the cups when she made the beds and cleaned the cabin. The men were collected by the car at 8:30 in the morning. They had the small cases. They were out all day and returned late. The manager thought they were businessmen and the cases contained samples. The next day they left at the same time in the morning but returned in the early evening. They checked out of the motel. Wayne Redmond paid in cash. The same car took them away. It might have been the same driver. They were killed the following morning.

They had a fair amount of luggage, some of which they did not unpack. The maid said that the luggage looked expensive. It was lightweight stuff, pretty new. She did not remember anything special about such of their belongings as she saw when she did the cabin the two mornings. One of the men had a navy-blue cashmere robe that she liked, but she did not know which man the robe belonged to and she did not look at the label. She said she had not herself spoken to either man but she was shocked that such recent guests should be dead.

The letter was typewritten on plain paper of a well-known brand. It gave no address or date. It said:

Dear Wayne,
Keep plugged in one more night then come along home. Unless, of course, you get a squeep on our client.
Stay cool,
Chuck.

The signature was handwritten with a ball-point. The envelope had no stamp or postmark, but nobody remembered it having been delivered by hand to the motel. Nobody knew what a "squeep" was.

Neither the name Wayne Redmond nor a photograph meant anything to the Schenectady police. There was no Wayne Redmond in the directory, the voters registration roll, or any other list. One store in the city identified the suit and another the shoes, but neither recognized the customer.

The General Motors dealer in Troy was the one whose truck salesman had been killed on his motorcycle. No one in the company knew Wayne Redmond's name or his face.

There was no trace in Boston of a J. R. Purvis. No one in the motel recalled having heard him speak, so it was unknown whether he spoke with a Bostonian accent. No Boston dentist identified the fillings and bridgework in his mouth.

The memory banks of the F.B.I. computers reported "Negative" to names, prints, and the one recognizable face.

There was no record of either gun. They were not registered. If they were stolen the thefts had not been reported. It was assumed they had been bought legally over the counter in one of the states where this was possible, or else smuggled into the country.

Every 1973 tan Chrysler with Vermont plates was checked. None had been near the All Seasons Motor Lodge. It was assumed that the plates were false.

Gabetti's widow took the news of her husband's death

stoically. She did not know about any $100,000 or $50,000, or any deals her husband had made in Pittsfield or Troy. She did not know if he had recently been to either town. He had a girl in some other town but she did not know where. When she asked him he clobbered her. She did not divorce him because she was a devout Catholic and she had no money. She had never heard of the Blue Hill Pilgrims. She said that her husband had been going straight for a long time, since before they were married. He was a heel but he was going straight. She did not think he had the brain to blackmail anybody, but he was heel enough.

The house was searched but nothing was found. It was quite a poor household although all the children were fat.

Camilla Cordle denied that there was anything in her late husband's private life about which he could have been blackmailed. She was evidently speaking the truth as she knew it. This could mean that there had been nothing shameful, or that David Cordle was tactful and secretive.

Nobody else in his household or family knew anything either. The state police were involved because of the deaths at the bottling plant, and they were not as reverential towards the Cordles as the Blue Hill force. But the lieutenant assigned to the investigation agreed with Fred Bailey that these people were truthful.

A Geoffrey Cordle was mentioned, a bachelor cousin recently deceased. The New York police reported that his death was entirely accidental. He was run over by a teenager who could hardly stand up for the whisky he had been drinking. The teenager had stopped and tried to help. But he was too drunk to help and Geoffrey Cordle was already dead. But Geoffrey was named by half a dozen people as the one individual in all David's circle about whose private life there might be a doubt.

He was checked out. It was easy. He was well known. His life was an open book and a very dull one. His manner had struck many people as effeminate, but if he was a praticing homosexual, or had any other kink, he was extremely discreet.

It thus became probable, though by no means certain, that three men had discovered a secret of Cordle's, possibly involving his late cousin, and had successfully blackmailed him. Why they had cut in Gabetti it was impossible to say.

86

Two of the men as well as Gabetti were dead. There was still a third man. It was possible that the third man had nothing to do with blackmail or with the killing of Gabetti.

The police tried very hard to get a description of a man who had been driving a tan Chrysler with Vermont plates. The car had been seen, but the driver had not been especially noticed at any gas station, store, motel, bar or anywhere else. The general impression was of a man in his 30s. Nobody knew if he was tall or short because he had never been seen except at the wheel of the car.

The only way he could be traced, if he was the survivor of a team of blackmailers, was by the check Dave Cordle had made out. The F.B.I. went to the Panamanian bank in New York. They were given full and immediate cooperation. An account had been opened at the bank, by mail, by a company with the registered name of Blue Hill Pilgrims, incorporated in the Bahamas. A check for $100,000 had been paid into this account and cleared by the Cordle Trust's bank. Three days later the money had been transferred by bank draft to Zurich and the account closed. The episode was strange but perfectly legal. The officer of the Blue Hill Pilgrims empowered to write checks was a Mr. Howard P. Curwen.

The F.B.I. took Mr. Curwen's specimen signature and correspondence which he had signed. The correspondence was fingerprinted but it carried no prints on the F.B.I.'s files. Persons named Howard P. Curwen in various cities were exonerated of any involvement.

The Bahamas government had records of the incorporation and subsequent liquidation of the Blue Hill Pilgrims. It was stated to be a property company. It had paid the necessary fees but it had never traded. Its registered address was in care of a bank which it had never used.

It might be possible to extract money from Switzerland and return it to the Cordle Trust, if fraud could be proved in the Swiss courts. It would probably not be possible to identify, by means of the money, the driver of the tan Chrysler. The real owners of ships jettisoning hundreds of tons of oil on to beaches were often impossible to discover, owing to nominees, cardboard companies, and the differing commercial laws of different countries: nobody expected to identify the new owner of Cordle's $100,000.

The Federal Aviation Administration completed its examination of the crash. They found that it had been caused by the failure of the tail assembly to answer the controls. The cable had been severed but it was impossible to say with certainty whether this had happened before or after the crash. The break might be cause or effect. If the cable had been severed before the crash, there was no evidence as to how this had happened. Other sections of the cable had been tested and were in good condition. The maintenance log was impeccably kept. Neither poor maintenance nor faulty manufacture was suspected.

At the same time there was no evidence of deliberate sabotage. The noise Mr. Tucker had heard in the fuselage of the aircraft was consistent with a very small explosive charge but also with a breakage under stress. No trace of a timing device had been found. No metal parts had been found which were inconsistent with components of the aircraft but consistent with a detonator.

"Seems that closes the case, like the guy said," said Colly.

"No," said Sandro. "Jenny is right."

"Am I?" said Jenny with surprise. "But I haven't said anything. Also I agree with Colly."

"If Gabetti was getting half, then those two men with false names and a false car had only $25,000 each."

"Very nice bread," said Colly.

"For that they put a little bomb which we do not understand in your airplane, kill a man in a way we do not understand in Troy and another in Pittsfield, kill Gabetti, and try to kill us."

"Plenty of gorillas would do that and more for twenty-five grand," said Colly.

"But these two were not backstreet heavies. They have good clothes. Their friend drives them in an expensive car. They have expensive luggage and one has a nice dressing gown."

"As to that friend," said Jenny. "I'm glad he doesn't know where we are."

"I also," said Sandro. "For a few days I cannot run after anybody or run away from anybody."

"Nor me," said Colly.

"You two stay put," said Jenny. "I'll do the running away for all of us."

"You have to protect us old *mutiles de la guerre,* darling," said Colly. "You better stand by the window with your squirrel rifle."

"Oh yes? How long for?"

"Around two weeks."

"Who's going to get your food, then?"

"You are. Only get it quick in case he sneaks up on us."

Jenny laughed. She looked out of the window, through the fine wire mesh which kept the mosquitoes out. A new moon had risen over the pond. It made a thin silver path across the mirror-smooth water. A fish or a bird, invisible, splashed in the water. The trees which girdled the pond were as still as a petrified forest in the windless evening. The moon was just above the treetops, hung on a sky of unbelievable purple. Jenny wondered if the wire screen in the window counted as glass by the terms of the nursery superstition. It was bad luck to see a new moon through glass. Would she get back luck, looking at it through the screen?

Sandro said: "Gabetti saw your car, *caro,* and remembered the number, and so he got out his big gun and came down to his office."

"Expecting to see me," said Colly. "Right."

"So. Why did those others come, early in the morning, with their guns?"

"They saw Colly's car too," said Jenny.

"Maybe. But why should they know it!"

"They happened to be passing and saw the light on."

"Or," said Colly, "they came to do like you. To search the joint."

"Where did they spend all the night?" said Sandro. "Why did they leave the motel when they were staying in the town?"

"How the hell should I know where they spent the night. Maybe they had girls. Maybe they had insomnia. Maybe they went to a party. What does it matter where two hoodlums, now dead, spent the night?"

"Maybe it does not matter," said Sandro. "But it is one more thing I do not understand. Where is the other, the man with the Chrysler?"

"Sneaking up," said Colly. "Get to that window, darling."

"Hey, wait," said Jenny. "Gabetti got Colly's name from Bertram Mills, yes?"

"Who, baby?"

"I mean Bernard Jones. The sweet one who kept falling over his feet. Gabetti got your name, as head snooper, from Jones. He told his friends, as they still were. The friends had Wilkins's office watched. They knew you'd go there in the end, because of what Jones was made to say. They followed you out of the place and tried to kill you. Then they lost you, when we came back here. So they looked you up in every book they could think of. They found out where you live and so forth, and the number of every car registered in your name. You're not at home in New York and you've left the hospital, but they've still got those car numbers. So they're looking for certain cars. So—"

"They check the numbers of every car they see, in every street in every place where they are?" said Sandro. "They look at every car in America in case one of them is Colly's?"

"Yes," said Jenny stoutly. "Or maybe Gabetti told them the number."

"Che scherzo."

"All right, but how do you answer your own question, you great fat useless Wop? Why *did* those two come to Gabetti's office in the dawn? Why *did* the chap poke a silenced pistol through the window? What brought them?"

"I do not know. There is something we have left out."

"You left the whisky out of this glass, darling," said Colly plaintively to Jenny. "And the ice."

As Jenny refilled Colly's glass she said: "Obviously we've left something out, but as everybody seems to be dead I don't see how we're going to find out what it is."

"Not everybody is dead," said Sandro. "I wish I knew who and where is the other man, the driver."

The other man, the driver, came slowly along the little country road. His tires crunched on leaves and pine branches but his engine made very little noise and he was driving without lights. His car was not a Chrysler. The Chrysler had recovered its own New York plates and it was safely in Rochester in the locked garage of its owner. The owner was not expected back from Acapulco for another week. No one knew the car had left the garage. The clock recorded no additional mileage. The owner would never know the car had been borrowed, and if he knew he would not know who the borrower was.

The driver switched on the radio of his car. He pressed one of several buttons on the panel below the radio. The radio said *squeep-squeep-squeep*. The noise became gradually louder as the car approached the cabin beside the pond.

The Cadillac was still there, then. The squeep was still taped under the rear bumper.

The driver had put the squeep there himself, four nights earlier, when they found the car outside Gabetti's house in Blue Hill. It was lucky these people used a distinctive car. It was lucky Gabetti had seen the car, and done a few sums correctly in his thick guinea head, and gone down to his office to see if somebody was having a look at it. It was lucky, too, that Gabetti had mentioned the car when he talked to the people he found in his office. The bug in the office had picked up his remark about the Caddy parked outside his house. After that it was easily identified. The driver and his friends had gone at once to Gabetti's house and found the car. Only one Cadillac was parked in that street in a run-down section at the edge of town. The driver had taped the squeep under the rear bumper.

They had listened to the bug, he and the other two, the moment the warning buzzer in the receiver told them there were people in Gabetti's office. It was something they had expected. Tucker had been taking trouble and spending money. He would not stop snooping now, and Gabetti's office was the obvious place for his friends to go. They had predicted a visit but they had expected it sooner. They had kept the channel open all the time, moving around near Blue Hill but staying within range of the bug.

The bug had been planted in Gabetti's office when they first called there to proposition him. This was normal procedure. It might never be needed. If all went well it would never be needed. But the boss insisted on being able to keep tabs on anyone he did business with. Especially low-grade characters like Gabetti. He might try to get smart, he might try all kinds of fool tricks. They would be able to listen in on him.

In this case it was not Gabetti trying to get smart but Tucker trying to get nosy which alerted them and made them glad of a bug there in the office. They heard Tucker's questions to Gabetti, and Gabetti's replies, which were perfectly satisfactory. Then Tucker talked to New York and that showed he was making serious efforts to snoop. He survived the air-wreck and he was still snooping. So the driver and his friends kept the channel open to the bug in Gabetti's office.

Nothing happened for several days and nights and they were beginning to think Tucker and his friends had given up. Then the buzzer alerted them and they all listened. They had not recognized the deep voice with a foreign accent or the limey girl's voice. But they knew who these people were. They were Tucker's friends. It was useful to listen in to them, because it showed how much they knew. They knew nothing. They were floundering around in the dark. It was funny to listen to them. They could search the cheesy little office all they wanted. There was nothing in Gabetti's office which led back.

When Gabetti got there the situation was no different. He was tough. There was no reason he should talk to these amateurs. Then he mentioned the car, the Cadillac parked outside his home. This was excellent. It was a great stroke of luck. Tucker had disappeared. He had come out of the hospital and climbed into a little airplane with his friends and disappeared. The airplane had not landed at any recognized commercial airport but on somebody's field or a high school football ground or a stretch of empty road. Tucker disappeared with his friends into the blue. It was a bad thing. It was not anybody's fault but it was bad to have lost him. Now here was his car, identified by Gabetti. They found it and put the squeep on to it. The squeep did not require a close tail. While the tiny battery lasted its signal was good for twenty miles in flat country. The signal might be blanketed by mountains, but in mountain country the tail could keep much closer without being seen. If he got too close the squeep would tell him by getting very loud. It would lead them to Tucker and they would finish the job.

Then Gabetti cracked and the situation changed. The

bug picked up the fright in his voice and the things he began to say. He was the kind of bully who can dish it out but not take it. He did not know much but he knew too much. Alongside what Tucker already knew, what he said could be dangerous.

The driver had therefore taken the only possible decision. He had sent the other two down to the office. He had himself stayed by the radio receiver. Somebody had to keep listening in.

What followed was unfortunate.

But, at the end of it all, the squeep was still on the Cadillac. It led the driver to the cabin by the pond. He watched. He waited for three days. There was plenty of time. He wanted time. He wanted to get everything foolproof and to cover his tracks. He sent away all his equipment, baggage, identification. There was nothing in the car except what he needed for tonight. The car could be traced only to himself in a phoney cover personality. If anything went wrong there was nothing which led back to headquarters.

He wanted time and he took it. He could not permit himself any more failures. He could afford to give himself time because Tucker had a leg and arm in plaster and the big man was still on crutches. They were staying put. The girl brought in plenty of groceries in a jeep. They were provisioned for at least another week. No doubt they thought they were convalescing. They thought they were absolutely safe, hidden, off the map. Even if they suddenly went away he would know about it. He would be able to follow them.

He was getting near the cabin. He turned off the road at a place he had picked. He stopped the car and backed. He turned round so that he was pointing back the way he had come. He parked the car off the road. It was dark. The baby moon had set.

The driver turned off the radio. He groped under the dashboard and threw another switch. This turned the radio back into a normal one, receiving only on the commercial wavebands. No one would see the switch under the dashboard, and no one would guess that the radio was itself a powerful squeep, as well as a shortwave receiver for squeeps and bugs. This was routine procedure in case things went wrong and somebody inspected the car. But the driver had made very careful and thorough preparations and he did not expect anything to go wrong.

He was near enough to the cabin to get a clear signal from the minibugs. But it was not worth listening. It did not matter what the people in the cabin did because they would all very soon be dead.

CHAPTER EIGHT

"What this drink needs," said Jenny, "is a bit of mint."

"Squeeze a little of my toothpaste in it, darling," said Colly. "It's a pretty minty dentifrice. That's one of the reasons I'm so nice to be near. There's plenty of other reasons, but that's one of them."

"I wouldn't touch your toothpaste with a bargepole," said Jenny coldly.

"I don't believe you have a bargepole. I don't believe you even know what a bargepole is."

"It's what I wouldn't touch your toothpaste with. I know exactly where there's a big clump of mint. At least I think it's mint. And I think I know where it is. By that little stream that comes down at the edge of the wood."

"That's poison ivy, darling."

Jenny laughed. She said: "I won't be long. I want mint for the potatoes as well. Mint for Sandro and me, poison ivy for you. Where's the bloody flashlight?"

But she could not find the flashlight. She shrugged and went out into the darkness. The door whispered shut behind her. She went down the wooden steps of the cabin on to the granite slabs which sloped down towards the lake.

It was warm and very dark. The moon was down. A drift of thin cloud almost obscured the light of the stars.

Jenny was invisible. She wore black cotton pants and a black sweater over her blue and white checked shirt. She had washed her hair earlier in the evening and it was not yet dry; she had swathed it in a darkly-patterned towel which encircled her head like a turban. She was soundless. Her dirty sneakers made no noise on the granite and she stepped gently down over the broken rock towards the lake.

Her eyes grew more and more used to the darkness. She came down to the edge of the water and it gleamed faintly in the reflection of the misty starlight. The water was absolutely calm. A fish, invisible, plopped twenty yards away in the water. Birds rustled in the scrub by the water and in the edge of the woods.

Jenny went carefully along the rocks at the edge of the lake. She did not want to sprain her ankle or to fall into the water. And for reasons which were obscure to her she did not want to make any sound. There was no objection to making a noise, however loud. She could play a trombone by the lakeside without disturbing anybody. But Jenny was disinclined to wake the sleeping birds, or startle the animals of the night. She went slowly and carefully, with no sound.

She came to the mouth of the stream at the edge of the wood. She worked her way cautiously upstream for a few yards over rocks and moss. There was a patch of thick undergrowth to her left, between the stream and the cabin. She thought the clump of mint was near the undergrowth at the edge of the wood. Her probing toe found soft vegetation by the stream. She squatted beside it and snapped her lighter. It was the mint. There was poison ivy also but this was the clump of mint. She picked a handful.

The flame of the lighter made her think of a cigarette. She groped in the other pocket of her pants, but she had left her cigarettes in the cabin. It was annoying but not important. They were not far away. She let the top of the lighter click back into position, extinguishing the small jet of methane. She straightened and started back towards the cabin.

Another fish splashed far out in the lake. A bird chuckled softly in the pine trees. There was no wind and no other sound. Jenny made no sound. There was a strong scent of balsam from a group of pines which had been cooked all day by the sun.

Jenny sniffed luxuriously. She smelled the balsam and the aromatic perfume of the crushed mint in her hand. She smelled something else. There was a foreign smell, an incongruous smell, just perceptible over the fresh natural smells of balsam and mint.

Jenny smelled gasoline.

Colly's Cadillac and the old jeep were parked on the far side of the cabin. The Cadillac smelled of leather, the jeep sometimes of oil. The smell of gasoline could not come from them. There was no other gasoline. They did not have any cans of it. They did not use it for cooking or a generator or any other purpose in the cabin. There were some kerosene lamps but they made a completely different smell.

Jenny had wanted a cigarette. If she had remembered to bring her cigarettes to the lakeside, her nose would have been full of the smell of tobacco and she would not have noticed the faint, pungent smell of the gasoline.

There was a very faint hissing noise. Even the slightest wind would have hidden the noise. The branches of the pine trees would have gently shifted and the pine needles whispered together. But there was no wind. If Jenny had been walking less carefully, making any noise as she walked, she would not have heard the noise, but she was making no sound and moving very slowly. If she had been singing or whistling she would not have heard the noise. Often she sang or hummed or whistled, when she was walking or lying in the sun, but the peace of the night had silenced her.

Few people, however quiet, would have heard the sound. It was very soft. It was not strange or discordant. But Jenny was as alert as a wild animal, as the deer and foxes of the woods, and her senses and responses were highly trained.

She did not recognize the hissing. It was no sound she knew. It puzzled her. She listened intently. The noise was discontinuous. It went on for about fifteen seconds, stopped for a few seconds, and started again. There was no other sound. The smell of gasoline was stronger. It got stronger as Jenny moved very carefully and quietly nearer to the cabin. She thought that she was moving towards the source of the smell, but also that there was more gasoline.

Jenny crept nearer. She was still clutching the mint but she had forgotten about it. Her antennae were vibrating. Something was strange and wrong. Somebody was near the cabin. It had to be so. If she had lit the cigarette she wanted he would have seen the glowing tip. But he had not seen or heard her. It might still be possible to find out what this was about and deal with it.

Jenny stopped and listened intently for a movement. She stared into the darkness for a movement, a gleam of reflected starlight, a person, an explanation of the hissing and the smell of gasoline. But there was no sound except the faint discontinuous hiss, repeated again and again, fifteen seconds of hiss and then a few seconds of silence. There was nothing to be seen. Jenny tried to account for the hiss. It was like vapour escaping from a small hole in a pipe. It was like that, but that was impossible. It was like insecticide being jetted at a fruit tree from a gardener's syringe. And the gaps between the hisses were like the syringe being filled up again.

The smell of gasoline was getting very strong. But Sandro and Colly would not smell it inside the cabin because of the cigarettes they were smoking and the meat and onions cooking on the range.

A syringe jetting a spray of gasoline over the roof and walls of the cabin. Somebody had crept up under cover of darkness and was doing this in order to burn them alive. He might very easily succeed very soon.

If Jenny shouted to the others to get out of the cabin the man would immediately light the giant and lethal bonfire he had prepared. Neither Colly nor Sandro could move quickly. In any case it would be a moment before they understood what she was getting at. In spite of all their training and experience they felt secure. They were not alert for any kind of attack. Although people had been trying to kill them they did not feel threatened here in the cabin. They were certain they had dropped off the map. They would be slow to realize that Jenny was telling them to limp and stumble and haul themselves out of the cabin because it was soaked with gasoline spray from a pump.

As soon as Jenny shouted the man would fire the gasoline. The cabin would go up like a torch and Sandro and Colly would die before they could get out.

If she went to the cabin door the man would see her. He would see the glow of light from inside when she opened the door. She would be a perfect target at that moment if he wanted to shoot her. At the same time he could fire the gasoline and kill the others, who were crippled and would be slow to get up out of their chairs.

Jenny stared into the darkness. There were patches of very deep shadow near the cabin, black against black, made by bushes and a jumble of rock. The hiss seemed to be coming from that extra blackness.

Jenny thought savagely. The man would not, from choice, ignite the gasoline until he had got away a little. His pump, whatever it was, might have dribbled some gasoline from its nozzle, there would inevitably be some gas left in the pump and in his cans and buckets, there must be some on his hands and clothes, there must be a lot of vapor about. He would get well clear, creeping away through the darkness, and then light the fire at long range. Perhaps he had some kind of tracer bullet, or a small incendiary grenade. If Jenny forced him into quick action, he would drop his pump, run backwards a few paces, and light the fire. He would be quite safe. Nothing could go wrong. Colly and Sandro were certain to die.

Why was he doing it like this? To leave no trace, of course. To manufacture an accident. The Cadillac and the jeep would burn. Their gas would explode. That would explain the chemical traces of gasoline in the ashes of the cabin and of Sandro and Colly and Jenny.

Also this was the best way of killing several people at once. If he tried to shoot all three of them he might get only one, or none, and he might be shot himself. This way he ran no risk of failure and no risk to himself.

The cabin was covered with gasoline. The man himself had plenty of gasoline. In between there might be a safe strip, a kind of fire lane, where no gas had fallen. Jenny might be able to start a fire where the man himself was without setting light to the cabin. She dismissed the idea as soon as it occurred to her. The risk was too great. The man's aim with the pump might not have been consistent in the dark, and the pump might not be fully efficient at the end of each jet. There was quite likely a little river of gasoline between the pump and the cabin, and flame would run along it as soon as there was a spark at either end.

Hiss. Pause. Hiss. He was still pumping. The air reeked of gasoline.

There was no other way into the cabin. If Jenny made a circuit and approached it from the back or the far side

99

there was no way she could get in, and no way she could get the attention of the people inside without alerting the enemy.

The one immense advantage Jenny held was that the man had no idea she was out of doors. He must have arrived after she had gone down to the lake to get the mint. Against this she was unarmed. She had nothing in her pockets except a cigarette lighter which she dare not use. She held only a bunch of mint. Round her were rocks and sticks. It was no good throwing a rock in the general direction of a man she could not see. Also it might strike a spark off another rock when it hit.

The only thing to do was to stalk and clobber the man, and do it very quickly before he used up his gasoline and withdrew to safety and started his holocaust. The huge drawback to this plan was that there might be more than one man. There might be more than two. If there were three men then Jenny, unarmed, would be unable to stop them. Faced with this possibility, Jenny examined all the alternative plans she could think of. She considered using the jeep or the Cadillac to try to run the killer or killers down. She considered creating a diversion that would cause the enemy to chase her. She did not think these or other alternatives would work. She thought she would be killed as well as Sandro and Colly. It had to be the stalk, and the wildcat attack launched at the throat. She had to hope there was only one man.

She thought there was only one. One other man was linked to the two anonymous killers at the bottling plant. And this merciless affair tonight had the look of a one-man operation. Two or more men, with guns, could do it more simply and quickly with their guns. It was one man alone who, determined on foolproof massacre, would take all this trouble with gasoline and pump.

Jenny fought down her doubts and decided to assume that she had one adversary. She set herself to stalk him.

She went down into a crouch. She dropped the bunch of mint, thanking it silently for being the cause of her outing. She groped forward with her hands. If she put her fingers where her feet were going to go, step by step, she would avoid stepping on any twig or dry leaf or loose stone.

She began to move. Although speed was vital it was even more vital that she get to the man and disable him before he knew she was there. If she lost surprise she lost the battle. Given any warning, any at all, he would be off. His tracer bullet or grenade, his burning arrow or dart, would fire the cabin.

Jenny's eyes were used to the darkness. Whatever was to be seen she could see. There was nothing to be seen. The enemy was invisible. His eyes must be used to the darkness too. Her clothes were black and her hair was covered but her face would show pale. She kept her head low and advanced like a hunting cat over the tumbled rocks towards the faint sound of hissing.

Hiss. Pause. Hiss. Still there. Still jetting the lethal fuel over the cabin.

Sandro and Colly might be wondering where she had got to. They would not worry. They were used to her whims and disappearances. They would assume that she had suddenly decided to swim, or climb a pine tree, or try to mesmerise a drinking deer in the beam of a light. They would not worry because they knew that no one knew where they were.

Close. The smell very strong. Plenty of spilled gasoline on the ground and the air thick with inflammable vapor.

Hiss. Pause. The pause filled with the almost inaudible gurgle of the pump recharging. Jenny could tell almost exactly where the man was although she could not see him.

She crept forward. The fingertips of her left hand found a piece of smooth, clean granite for her foot. The stone was warm from the day's sun. The fingertips of her right hand explored the brittle fringes of a blueberry bush. She found a safe and silent landing for her right foot and advanced another half-yard. Her knees were groaning with the awkwardness of this long, cramped crawl. The toweling turban was hot and uncomfortable on her head, and kept nudging down into her eyes, but it was necessary to keep it on. She was still stiff and tender from the fight in the bottling plant.

She knew exactly what to do but she must be near enough and see well enough to do it. She must know where his head was and his throat and solar plexus. Those were the points to attack. She must know what was in his hands and whether it could form a weapon to smash down on her head when she went in. It would be nice to know a lot more but those things were essential.

101

She inched forward. She kept her face low to the ground and tilted down so as to reduce as far as possible the pale area. She moved very slowly. Speed was still vital but she was close now and she had to move very slowly and carefully. She controlled her breathing so that she made no noise in her nose or throat even though she was tired and would have liked to take deep breaths of the night air. Her heart was thudding with fright and excitement; it sounded inside her head as though it must be audible clear across the lake, but she knew this was an illusion.

Hiss. Pause. The faint gurgle. More gas in the pump. Hiss. More gas on the cabin. How many gallons had he sprayed on to the cabin? How had he brought all that gas down to the side of the cabin? Several trips from his own car left safely up the trail. Plastic jerricans, like the ones people used in motor boats. He could either take the empty jerricans away with him, or let them burn. They would arouse no suspicion if they were found in the ashes of a house where there were two cars.

Jenny's back ached and she was frightened of cramp in her calves and feet. She strained her eyes, furiously concentrating, staring into the darkness. The man was ten or twelve feet away, no more. But he was invisible.

Jenny saw the jet of gasoline arch up out of the midst of the thickest darkness and bedew the roof of the cabin. She followed the curve of the jet down to its source. That and the hiss pinpointed the nozzle of the pump. It was not enough.

It was a thin fine jet the pump was throwing. That was why he was taking so long. Why? Why not a bigger pump? Obviously because this one was silent. Because the fine spray made no noise when it landed on the roof of the cabin. Because he could manage this little pump on his own. Because it was in itself innocent, something used by thousands of law-abiding householders to spray their roses or fruit trees or currant bushes.

Jenny crept nearer: left fingertips, left toe, right fingertips, right toe: stop and look and listen.

There was a tiny sniff ahead. Nine feet ahead. The man sniffed. It was very quiet and brief, a little involuntary inhalation. Jenny would not have heard it a few feet further away but she heard it now. It told her where the man's head was. She stared at the sound, and she could see the

102

man. Now that she knew exactly where to look she could see him.

He was alone.

He was kneeling on one knee, facing to the left, toward the cabin. His left knee was on the ground, his right raised and bent. He was leaning his right elbow on his knee and holding the barrel of the syringe in his right hand. He was pushing the plunger of the long syringe with his left hand. Jenny could just distinguish the slow forward movement of his left arm as he pushed the plunger home into the back of the syringe.

Hiss.

He lowered the syringe. Some kind of tube went down into a big plastic gas tank by his knees. He pulled out the plunger of the syringe. Jenny heard the faint gurgle as the gasoline ran up the tube into the barrel of the syringe.

Jenny thought the syringe was made of dull brass. It would be an excellent weapon for bringing down on to her head.

The best thing would be to knock the man out with a rock from behind. But he was unapproachable from behind. He was backed against a tangle of little scrawny bushes. They would not be difficult to get through, but they would be impossible to get through silently.

Hiss. Gurgle.

Jenny thought the syringe would be a less effective weapon in the man's hands when it was at its longest— when the plunger was fully extended backwards. Also the man would be most preoccupied at the beginning of a new jet of gasoline, because of the necessity of aiming his nozzle at the roof or wall of the cabin.

Any second now.

The imminence of action, as always, made Jenny shudder. Her hands felt hot and her face cold. She was frightened for the others and she was very frightened for herself. The others were sitting under a volcano, and they could not move quickly enough to get out of its way once it was lit. She had to fight, but she did not want to be smashed on the head with the heavy brass tube, or to be burned alive. She was very excited. Her heart thudded in her throat, almost stifling her, and it took great effort to breathe quietly.

She was in the crouched position of a sprinter on his

starting blocks. She was waiting for the gun.

A bird chuckled sleepily a few yards away. A mosquito whined round Jenny's head. She felt the minute impact as it landed on her cheek, and the tiny poisoned prick of its mandibles. There was nothing she could do about it.

Gurgle. The syringe was full, the plunger fully extended. The man raised the syringe and aimed it at the roof of the cabin.

Jenny jumped.

She jumped in a flat dive, left arm extended and right crooked. The man would turn his head involuntarily towards her at the first movement. She hoped to get a straight finger jab into his eye with her left. Then she would chop with the heel of her right hand at his throat.

The fingers of her left hand jabbed into his eye. There was a shocking pain in her fingers but the pain in his eye would be worse. At the same moment her right hand came across with the chop. It was inaccurate and hit the side of his jaw. A split second later she landed half on top of the man and knocked him over on to the flat rock. He had flailed round with the syringe, aiming at Jenny's chest with the plunger. As she landed on top of him her weight pushed the plunger and emptied the syringe over the man's torso and face. She chopped again for the windpipe and the man grunted. He grabbed for her but she wriggled clear and tried to jump down with both heels on his groin. He flailed sideways with his legs and with the syringe and knocked over the plastic gas tank. She was on the top of him again, jabbing and chopping at his eyes and throat. The gasoline spewed over them both.

The man was grunting and madly struggling. He was not a big man but he was stronger than Jenny. But she was more expert at fighting. The man was desperate and quite strong but he was not a fighter. The clothes of both of them were soaked in gasoline and they choked in the fumes. Jenny gouged at an eye and the man screamed like a rabbit but now he was hitting her with something. His flailing hand had found a gun and he was hitting her with the butt. He connected on her wrist. She sobbed and let go of his throat. He pulled away from her, kicking out violently with his feet. One of his feet connected with her face and she keeled over backwards. He scrambled clear and got to his feet. He began to run, shambling away from

Jenny and from the spilled gas tank.

He would stop and turn and fire at the cabin and at her, both sodden with gasoline.

Jenny gasped with effort and pain and hurled herself forward again in a dive. She grabbed at the man's ankles and caught one of them. He staggered and came down. His gun hand hit the ground and the gun tinkled away over the rocks. Jenny dived for the gun and got it. It was unusually big, long and fat and surprisingly light. It was not a kind of gun she had met before. She swiveled it towards the man. He knew she had got the gun. He screamed. He tried to struggle to his feet and run.

Jenny fired.

The off gun was a Very pistol. The report was not loud. A ball of white fire shot lazily at the man and hit him on the thigh. It lit the gasoline which soaked the man's clothes and in a second he was a screaming, struggling human torch.

Jenny shuddered and turned away. She felt sick. She could hardly move for pain and horror and nausea.

In a moment fire would be everywhere, because the spilled gas was everywhere. It was all over the cabin and all over her and all over the ground, the rocks and dry bushes.

Jenny managed to get to her feet. She stumbled towards the cabin. As she went she pulled off her reeking, sodden sweater and shirt and pants. Her underwear was bound to have absorbed a little gasoline but not so much. Her shoes were soaked in it. She pulled them off. Barefooted, in bra and bikini pants, she stumbled up the steps of the cabin.

"Upsidaisy," she said.

Colly and Sandro looked up in stupefaction. They had not heard the pop of the Very pistol against the murmur of Colly's radio, the cooking noises from the range, and their own desultory conversation. They had not smelled the gasoline over their cigarettes and bourbon and the onions in the pan on the range. They had not wondered very deeply about Jenny's prolonged absence.

Now they saw Jenny standing in the door of the cabin, almost naked, dirty, disheveled, panting and sobbing, bleeding from a cut on her cheek and one on her wrist and from grazes and cuts on her thighs and knees and arms.

After a moment of numbed amazement they began to obey Jenny's order to get out of the cabin. They groped for crutches. Sandro hobbled out on his own. Jenny supported Colly, grabbing a few belongings with her other hand. They made it down the steps of the cabin on to the granite.

"Oh my God," said Colly.

The man who was on fire was trying to run towards the haven of the lake. He did not make it. He teetered and fell forward on to his knees. He was screaming with the high drone of an oboe. It was amazing that he was still alive.

They watched aghast. There was nothing they could do.

Flames, like little predatory animals, began to run from the blazing torch of the man towards the cabin.

"*Andiamo,*" said Sandro calmly.

They stumbled awkwardly, as quickly as they could, down the sloping granite towards the edge of the lake.

The burning man fell forward on to his face.

The first of the invading flames arrived at the gasoline-soaked timbers of the cabin. Flame shot up the sides of the cabin. The front of the cabin was striped with vertical lines of flame and suddenly it was a single roaring wall of flame and a great flame exploded upwards from the roof. The three by the lakeside felt a blast of heat from the burning gasoline.

"Cars," said Colly.

Sandro shrugged.

Jenny said: "I think I want a wash."

She subsided into the cool safe water of the lake, and turned her face away from the burning cabin and the burning remains of the man she had killed.

CHAPTER NINE

At dawn there was no cabin and there were no cars but the fire was still burning.

The roughly-cemented lumps of local stone which had been the foundations of the cabin were all that stood upright. The cement had split and crumbled and some of the rocks had exploded in the intense heat of the fire at its height, but the foundations still stood, incomplete and blackened and untidily crowned with still-burning fragments of the cabin. Inside the shell of the foundations, and outside for a few yards in all directions, incandescent ash was heaped, glowing balks of wood still incompletely consumed, split and blackened pieces of pottery, molten blobs of glass, drifting cobwebby ash of fabric, and the almost vaporized remains of civilized life in a decent dwelling.

The burned-out shells of the cars behind the cabin were the ugliest part of the mess.

There were no trees near the cabin, and only a sprinkling of low scrubby bushes. Most of these bushes had been destroyed but the woods were safe. All the trees were far enough back from the cabin. The nearer trees had been chopped down to build the cabin or to provide firewood. It was lucky the night had been windless and the flame and heat almost perfectly vertical.

There was not much left of the dead man. He had smelled horrible while he cooked but now he was burned clean. The body was near enough to the cabin for the intense heat of the fire to keep it incandescent until there was nothing except a few pieces of metal and the larger bones.

Jenny cleaned herself up in the lake. She washed the blood off her face and body. She dried herself on a sweater of Sandro's which she had grabbed as they escaped out of the cabin. She also had some khaki slacks of Colly's. She put these on and rolled up the legs. She put on the huge damp sweater. She had no shoes. She washed her checked shirt in the lake. There was not much gasoline in it because she had been wearing a sweater. It was the single survivor of all her clothes and she felt sentimentally attached to it.

Colly had jarred his broken leg a little, in spite of the plaster and in spite of Jenny's help, coming down over the granite to the lakeside. Sandro had fallen, putting his crutch down on a loose stone in the dark. He pretended to the others that falling on his wound had not bothered him but it hurt very badly for a time.

There were a few cigarettes. There was nothing to drink. There was nothing to eat. None of them had a comb. The men had no razors. Colly had a handkerchief and a pack of Chesterfields. Jenny had nothing. None of them had any money, checks, credit cards, or identification.

"But we're alive," said Jenny weakly.

"Yes," agreed Colly. "Which reminds me. In case I forget, which I probably will, thanks."

"Grazie, amore," rumbled Sandro.

Colly and Sandro both kissed Jenny with gratitude and love.

Jenny smiled. She pushed the wet hair back from her forehead. She said: "Now that it's getting light I'll go and look for his car."

"Watch out for the prickles, baby."

"If my feet get sore I'll walk on my hands."

"Don't bring the car very near," said Sandro.

Jenny set off. She went round the pyre of the cabin. It still gave off a terrific heat and a few yellow-white flames still flickered busily among the incandescent ash of the wood and the red-hot stone. Jenny made a wide detour round it, and started up the dirt road looking for the car.

She felt all right. The water of the lake had been a godsend, both at the time of the fire and in the dawn. Her shirt and underwear would dry when the sun came up. These funny clothes would feel more comfortable when

108

she had something on underneath them. They would still look absurd—rolled-up pants billowing round her hips, and Sandro's sweater like a tent for an elephant—but they would be less scratchy. The dead man had not much damaged her face or wrist, and her other injuries were superficial. She was stiff and sore but no worse than that.

The sky brightened. It was another beautiful, windless day. It would be hot.

Jenny saw the car. It was a good one, fairly new, a black four-door Oldsmobile. It was dusty from the country roads. It had New York plates. It was parked off the track, pointing away from the cabin.

Jenny walked over the rough, spiny ground to the car. It was locked. That would not detain them long. There was a light raincoat in the back seat but no visible luggage or papers.

The identification disc said that the car belonged to J. L. Cork. J. L. Cork no longer required his car. It would do to get them into the village.

She had nothing to pick the lock of the car with so she started back stiffly to the others.

Sandro made it to the car and opened the door. They collected Colly. They went to the village. Colly told Jenny to park the Oldsmobile inconspicuously among other cars. Jenny did not understand but she obeyed. They went to the police. Colly did the talking.

Colly said he had knocked over a polythene bottle of gasoline with which he was trying to clean some oil off a pair of white linen pants. He was awkward because of the plaster on his arm. That was why he knocked over the bottle. At the same time he knocked over an ashtray which had a lighted cigarette on it. The cigarette started a fire in the spilled gas. They tried to put the fire out. But the fire spread and they got out of the cabin.

The police were concerned about the fire, which had not been seen by the forest rangers because the lake was low down in a little steep circle of hills. It was not a place of high fire-risk because the trees were nearly all hardwood, not pine. The rangers would get out there at once.

"Why?" said Jenny afterwards.

"Because," said Colly, "I want to get out of here. I want to climb into a car nobody ever saw before and go a long way away."

109

"We don't usually jump into other people's cars and run," said Jenny.

"No, baby. But I don't usually have broken arms and legs, and Sandro doesn't usually go around with perforations in his thigh."

"But the car. We can't take this car."

"This car is exactly what we can take. Think, darling. Those guys at the bottling plant. Phony personalities, totally untraceable, nothing leading anywhere. J. L. Cork doesn't exist either, except as a name to buy the car and pay the tax on it. We're not depriving the police of anything except a headache. There won't be any useful prints in the car. There isn't anything in the car at all."

"The coat?"

"No name, no laundry mark, a branded item sold nationally. Normal size. Fits me pretty well. I'm glad to have the coat, as I don't have anything else."

"I might borrow it."

"Ask nicely."

"But what about the man?" said Jenny. "Alias J. L. Cork? What about his remains?"

"He doesn't have any remains."

"Bones."

"We dropped them a long way out in the lake."

"*What?*"

"While you were finding his heap."

"But why?"

"Because we don't want to hang around for any more inquests, telling the world we're alive and well and waiting to be shot at."

"Inquests are not so terrible," said Jenny. "We could find another place to stay—"

"Giving the police our address."

"Well, of course. Why not?"

"Who knew where we were? Who in the whole state of Vermont, the whole goddam union, apart from a few people in the village here? They only know my name, which is a pretty common name. They don't know anything about you. Outside of the Blue Hill police—"

"Oh, darling. Not Fred Bailey. Don't tell me—"

"I don't tell you anything. But a leak from his office is a possibility. It has to be. That's why I want to travel in a car they can't possibly tie to us."

110

"That is all quite right," said Sandro.

"Well," said Jenny, "I've never known us break so many laws all at the same time."

Colly established his identity sufficiently to raise some money. They bought a few things. They set off in the car. Nobody saw them get into the car or drive away in it. They headed south.

After a time Jenny said: "Why are we running away when it's finished?"

"Do we know it's finished, baby?"

"Of course it is."

"There are still many questions," said Sandro.

"Like," said Colly, "why did the blackmailers use Gabetti? How did they know what airplane I was taking from New York? Why did they happen to call on Gabetti in the middle of the night? Why only two of them, when they had three? How did they kill a machinery broker in one town and a truck salesman in another town? How did J. L. Cork find our cabin?"

"I don't know the answer to a single one of those idiotic questions," said Jenny, "and I'm not going to try."

"Their intelligence was pretty good," said Colly thoughtfully. "And they made themselves pretty anonymous."

"So?"

"So that's not easy. Nowadays you trail your personality around with you wherever you go. A bum in a gutter can lose his identity, but a man with money, a car, clothes, credit facilities, needing somewhere to sleep . . ."

"A man can construct a false personality. It's not impossible."

"Of course not, darling. These people did it. But they were very professional about it. Very effective and organized."

"So?"

"So that's another puzzle. It doesn't tally with the raid on Gabetti's. God Almighty, darling, professionals would have killed Sandro and you. A professional would have split your skull with that syringe and barbecued Sandro and me."

"So?"

"So Holmes is baffled."

"Anche me," said Sandro. "There is much puzzle but

111

until we are quite well I think we must forget the puzzle."

"Drop out of sight," said Jenny, "and play three-handed bridge?"

"We thought we dropped out of sight at the pond," said Colly. "Let's do it properly this time."

"Are you scared they'll come again, darling? Who is there to come again?"

"Well, we don't actually know the two third men are the same third man, do we?"

"I expect I could make sense of that," said Jenny, "if I wasn't concentrating on the road."

"Look, there was a third man in Blue Hill, the mysterious driver. And there was your friend with the syringe. He might not be the same man, is all I'm saying."

"Of course he is. He must be."

"Maybe, maybe not. Maybe he has more friends still."

"Well, all right," said Jenny, "but if there is one of them left, we haven't the slightest idea who he is."

"That's right. That's worrying, don't you think?"

"But as long as we don't know who he is, we can't do him any harm, can we? How do we threaten him? Why should he bother with us? Why should he take the risk of trying to do us in when there's not the slightest need?"

"I don't know," said Colly. "I think he just might."

"Just to be spiteful?"

"Just to be safe."

"All right," said Jenny. "Then we'll go to Mexico."

"In this heat? Are you crazy?"

"I wanted to stay in Vermont. Failing that I want to go to Mexico. I want to practice my Spanish."

"Okay okay. Mexico. You're the only one who can drive so we better go where you want."

"I knew you'd agree."

"I must be out of my mind. What do you think, Sandro?"

But Sandro was asleep.

Two men sat in a Buick on a road outside Harrisburg in Southern Pennsylvania. One dictated a report into a tape recorder. He described, in brisk and factual terms, what they had achieved in the last two days. He summarized what they had learned and what they expected to learn during the following week. The other man meanwhile checked some items of sophisticated, miniaturized electronic equipment; he packed them away into slots in a leather-covered executive briefcase.

The two men were similar in appearance and not far apart in age. The one with the tape-recorder, who was in the driver's seat, was a year or two under thirty. His companion was a year or two over thirty. They were neat, executive types, college men. They looked as if they preferred Burgundy to bourbon, Mozart to rock, and figuring to fighting.

The first man completed his report and signed off. He snipped the tape, wound the recorded footage back, and took the spool off the recorder. He put the spool into a reinforced envelope with a printed address and prepaid postage.

Then he groped under the radio of the car. He found a switch. Only someone who knew it was there would have suspected the existence of the switch. He threw the switch. He pressed one of the buttons on the panel below the radio. This would normally have brought him Country and Western music from a local radio station, but since he had operated the hidden switch under the radio it brought him a different signal on ultra short wave. It brought him the *squeep-squeep* of the trail-bug they had attached to a car in the parking lot of an industrial laboratory in Harrisburg.

He pressed a different button. It brought him a voice, faint but comprehensible. It was the voice of a man dictating a letter. The letter accepted an invitation to speak at a seminar on petrochemistry in Baltimore.

"Nice signal," said the man with the briefcase on his lap.

"Yes. Pretty near extreme range."

The younger man pressed a third button on the panel below the radio. He got another mechanical signal, lower-toned than the first.

"One of ours," said the older man, surprised. "Who's around here?"

The signal was discontinuous. It came in longs and shorts in a recurring pattern.

The younger man took out a notebook and looked at a typed list pasted to one of the pages.

"304," he said. "The Olds. That's Morton's car."

"Morton's in Vermont.'

"His car is around seventy-five miles away.'

113

"It can't be."

"Listen."

"Yes, you're absolutely right. Stolen, maybe. We'd better get to a telephone."

The younger man drove the Buick in towards the center of Harrisburg. It was very hot. People who could afford it were all away. He stopped near a big drugstore. There were quite a few people in the drugstore and the soda fountain was crowded. The other man waited for the telephone in the drugstore. The store was air-conditioned. The air felt clammy after the dry heat of the road. His drip-dry shirt clung damply to his back. Two high school boys on vacation were helping the regular soda jerk at the long counter of the fountain. The man bought a Coke and waited in a line for the telephone.

The driver waited in the Buick. He listened to the discontinuous, rhythmic signal from the radio of the Olds. It was a much more powerful signal than the regular squeep, since it used parts of the car radio and ran off the car's battery. The signal was transmitted automatically whether the radio was in use or not, and regardless of which waveband the receiver was turned to. It was a precaution. All the company's cars carried their own high-powered squeeps in case of trouble.

The older man came out of the drugstore. His face was worried. He got in beside the driver.

He said: "Tucker has Morton's car."

"How the hell does the office know that?"

It doesn't. But it has to be Tucker and his friends in that car. They disappeared and the car disappeared and Morton disappeared, all at the same time."

"Did they kill Morton?"

"Seems so."

"Well, they finally got unlucky. Of all the cars in the world to choose."

"Yes, we can finish it now. As long as they don't find that radio."

"They wouldn't find that in a hundred years."

"They did pretty well so far."

"Yes."

"One of us has to stay here. I'll find a place near the lab and keep plugged in. The office will send somebody down with another car."

"And me?"

"Follow the Olds. Wait for help before you hit. George Collins is on his way from Cincinnati. He'll give you a cross bearing as soon as he picks up the squeep."

"Collins. Good. Okay, I'll listen out for him."

"Tucker won't be heading back north, if he came all this way south. He's going west towards Pittsburgh, southwest into the mountains, or south into Maryland."

"He might go east or west of the mountains. The squeep won't get across the Alleghenies."

"George will pick him up pretty soon."

"Can I reach George?"

"Channel B."

"Christ."

"I know, but the office says this is an emergency. Don't talk more than you have to. Just enough to get coordinates and home on the Olds."

"Suppose Tucker and his friends have split up?"

"No way. Only one's in shape to drive. Good luck, Bill."

George Collins drove east from Cincinnati. He was worried in case Tucker kept due south and traveled fast. The mountains would blanket even the powerful squeep of the Oldsmobile's radio.

The girl beside him kept the squeep channel open. She had the volume of their radio turned up full.

Collins was huskier than the men in the Buick, but he was of similar age and type. Like them, he was the evident product of an Eastern University, but one who had gone out for football or crew.

The girl looked like a Vassar girl. She looked twenty-eight and serious. She looked virginal although she wore a wedding ring.

She said suddenly: "That's it!"

"Are you sure?"

The girl listened intently and checked with a notebook. The rhythmic signal was faint but it could be followed.

She said: "Yes. About a hundred miles."

"I think they're coming west. Talk to Bill."

"Want to stop?" asked Jenny, looking across with concern at Colly. His voice had been cheerful but his face showed signs of pain and fatigue.

115

"Well, yeah," he admitted. "I'm stiff as hell. And you must be tired, darling."

"Bushed. Not Sandro, though. Wake up, fat Wop! You've been asleep for two hundred miles."

Sandro grunted and sat up in the capacious back seat of the Oldsmobile. *"Dove siamo?"*

"Guthrieville, West Virginia," said Colly. "I never heard of it either. Jenny picked this route, and you were snoring so loud I didn't have the strength to argue."

"I wanted to see these mountains," said Jenny, "and drink moonshine whisky, and hear a mountain dulcimer, and get caught up in a feud."

"What will happen here, baby, is you'll drink drugstore rye, hear a jukebox, and get caught up in a parade of local Kiwanis."

They were coming down into a narrow valley in the early evening. Hills to the west blocked out the sunset and cast heavy blue shadows into the valley. The higher hills to the east were a menacing purple against the darkening sky. The country seemed steeper and wilder than Vermont; it was at the same time somewhat slovenly. There were groups of ruined shacks and messy, abandoned mine workings. The small town ahead of them in the valley glared with meretricious neon in the gathering darkness.

"There," said Jenny. "Lit up like a Christmas tree. Look what a lovely place I've found for you."

"Of all the crazy ways to get from Vermont to Mexico," said Colly.

"Travel broadens the mind. Even yours. This may not be the quickest way, but it's not very far round. Besides, we're off the map."

"We're off any map *I* want to use."

"Then it is a good place for us," said Sandro. "We stop. I want very much food."

"We'll find hamburgers," said Colly dubiously. "I guess you may have to settle for very much hamburger."

Jenny slowed down in the main street of Guthrieville. It had a ghost town look. Its relevance had disappeared. Its prosperity had been short-lived. Guthrie had chosen badly. His town had never been an overnight bonanza shanty-town, like the El Dorados and Silver Cities of the West, or built itself on a hillside of solid coal, like other towns in

116

West Virginia and Eastern Pennsylvania.

There was no motel.

"Let's get on," said Jenny. "By morning we can be in Memphis."

"Not on these roads," said Colly. "Not with you as tired as you are, baby. Not with Sandro grumbling about food."

"Drink also," said Sandro.

"Yes," Jenny agreed, "I could do with some of that."

The Guthrieville Hotel was a gaunt, ill-lit building in the middle of town. Its hall was by Norman Rockwell, with dark varnished wood, framed prints after Maxwell Parrish, and a dark clerk in a green eyeshade. There were plenty of vacant rooms in the hotel.

To save trouble when they registered, Sandro said he was Mr. Ganz, Jenny said she was Miss Norrie, and Colly said he was Mr. Tucker.

"No food here, folks," said the clerk. "Cook has the shingles. Recommend Antoines, three blocks south."

They went through the sad little town to a restaurant which, if ever French, had long since reverted. The hamburgers were perfectly all right and so was the rye whisky. The coffee was terrible.

"They would stay in a place where there's only the one place to stay," said the girl who looked like a Vassar girl.

"We don't dare check in at the same hotel, Debbie."

"No."

The two company cars were parked four miles north at the head of the narrow valley. Bill had got out of the Buick and sat behind George Collins and the girl.

The girl said: "Can't we do it tonight?"

"In the hotel? A shoot-out in the street?"

"At least we wouldn't be stuck here in these cars."

George Collins said: "Morton reported what happened at that factory in Blue Hill."

"This is not my bag," said Bill unhappily. "I think we need more help."

"Ah, Christ," said the girl contemptuously.

"As a matter of fact I think Bill is right," said George Collins. "The office does not want any more mistakes. Any more casualties. The only way to be certain is to have two, three, maybe four more people."

"It's all wasting time," said the girl. "We ought to be in Cincinnati and Bill ought to be in Harrisburg."

"First things first," said George Collins. "We have to kill these people."

When it was full dark he drove to the edge of town. He called from a bar. He left a message and the number of the bar with the night operator in the office. He had a drink while he waited for the return call.

The office called back. He answered in monosyllables.

He paid for his drink and call and went out to the car. He turned it and rejoined the others at the head of the valley.

He said: "We're in luck. Five people are coming from Washington in two cars."

"Men?"

"Three men. Two girls. Joe Steel in charge."

"What's Steel been doing in Washington with a platoon like that?"

"Seems a United States Senator is having it off with a black chiropractor."

"Fine. Let's hope he's a rich Senator."

"Let's hope," said George Collins sourly, "he doesn't jump off the top of the Capitol and land us with another damned Galahad."

"Can Joe meet us tomorrow?" asked the girl.

"Yep."

"Then we could be all through by this time tomorrow night?"

"Yes."

"Why, actually," asked the girl, as though the question had for the first time occurred to her, "do we have to kill these people?"

"Because any minute now they're going to wake up," said George Collins.

"Beautiful dreamers, wake unto what?"

"Wake unto what it is they know. Nobody else knows it, or we wouldn't be here."

"Ah."

"Nobody else knows it, and it seems that they don't know they know it yet. But any minute now it's perfectly possible they'll be in a position to blow the whole company apart."

"Ah. Well, we don't want that."

"No, dear."

"So let's go ahead and kill them."

"That's right, Debbie. Let's do that."

"Frankly," said Bill, "This is not my bag."

CHAPTER TEN

Guthrieville was very quiet all night. It was even quieter than Blue Hill. No cars or trucks thundered through. No songs were sung. Men who got drunk did so in morose silence.

Jenny slept well. She was tired after the long drive. Neither Sandro nor Colly slept well because they were both in some pain. They were not bitten in the night by any fleas or bedbugs. Breakfast was abominable.

Colly wanted to start at 11 but they started at 8:30. Sandro sat beside Jenny in the front of the Oldsmobile.

They went southwest through the West Virginia mountains. The high spine of the Alleghenies blocked out part of the sky to the east.

By noon it was very hot. They were nearly into Kentucky. They were safe. Probably they had no remaining enemies. But if any of their enemies survived, the survivor did not know where they were.

George Collins kept quite close to the Olds. Most of the time the squeep was very loud though sometimes the signal was blanketed by the hills. Bill followed him in the Buick from Harrisburg. Debbie rode with George. She was impatient to kill the three in the Olds as she had more important things to get back to in Cincinnati.

Joe Steel and his party had come fast and far. They had gone round by the south. Now they had turned up northwards on one of the roads to the west of the main ridge of the mountains. The distinct rhythms of their squeeps were not as loud, to George and Debbie, as the squeep of the Olds, but they were getting louder.

Behind the Olds were two cars and three people. In front of it were two cars and five people. The eight people closing in on the Olds were under strict orders to kill, without fail, today and not tomorrow, the three people in the Olds, one of whom had two fractured limbs and another a bullet wound in the thigh.

Jenny drove through a few small towns. The little roads which Jenny had picked which Sandro followed on a map on his knee, did not go near big towns. In the big towns neon and car horns might have seemed at home. But in the forgotten small towns, on the untidy western slopes of the mountains, neon and horns seemed a claim without foundation, a spurious badge of membership.

"*Son stanco*," said Sandro. "I will shut up my eyes for 20 minutes."

"You're not tired, you're just lazy," said Jenny. "Read the bloody map."

"No need. There is no road except this road for many miles. From this place to a place called Anderson there is no other road."

"It's a long lane that has no turning," grumbled Colly from the back. "Suits me. You put the heap round the turns so goddam fast, Jenny, you throw me around like a pea in a big drum."

"Sorry, darling. I'll try and throw you around like a pea in a little drum."

Sandro was right. This section of the mountains was so empty that there were no towns to turn off the road to. There was no traffic. It was not clear why a road had ever been built between Wayne's Crossing and Anderson. Nobody went from one town to the other. Nobody wanted to visit either place, but only to leave. Some county politician had once bought votes in the mountains with the promise of this road; his brother had grown rich building the road; it was a bad, narrow road serving no purpose.

It was a nasty stretch of road. Not scenically. It was all right scenically, in the empty grandeur of the Southern Alleghenies. But Jenny disliked a road without turnings. She disliked being deprived of options. You were like someone on rails, someone on the Cresta run. The thought

121

of a road like an optionless *piste* for miles before and behind sent a small uneasy shiver up her spine. This was neither instinct nor superstition, but experience. A road with no outlets, in empty country, was the world's most perfect trap.

The last enemy had fried to nothing, like a marshmallow dropped in a campfire, on the edge of the Vermont trout pond. They were out of sight, they must be. But there were still nagging unanswered questions, a lot of questions, too many questions. Jenny drove fast to get to Anderson and to a road with intersections and alternatives.

Joe Steel had divided his party to get a cross bearing on the squeep. They rejoined in Anderson. Joe turned north on the single intersection in the middle of Anderson. The other car dropped in behind. The squeeps of the Olds were loud and getting louder. The squeeps of the cars following the Olds were loud.

They stopped three miles north of the town. Joe picked the place because of a rock beside the road and the way the road curved to the north. They parked the second car on the shoulder of the road. They turned the other and parked in the middle of the road. The cars were almost side by side. The second car blocked the shoulder and the two cars together blocked the road to any vehicle coming from either direction.

George Collins had difficulty keeping up with the Olds after Wayne's Crossing. Before that it had been traveling at a reasonable speed, but now the driver in front was breaking all the laws and the Olds was a fast car.

The squeeps from Joe Steel's two cars were almost as loud as the others. They were four miles out of Anderson.

"Get on," said Debbie. "You have to close up."

"Yeah. But we don't want corpses before we're ready."

"Trouble," said Jenny.

She braked hard when the parked cars came into view 150 yards away.

"More behind," said Colly.

Sandro woke up. He looked back and forward. He took his gun out of the dashboard, the new gun which replaced the one lost in the burned cabin.

Jenny stopped the Oldsmobile by the side of the road. She stopped just outside effective pistol range from the parked cars, unless the people in the cars were very good shots.

There was no room to get by on the right of the car in the road. A big lump of rock like an Easter Island statue rose just back from the roadside. There was no room to get by on the left. A car parked on the dirt shoulder of the road blocked the way. At the edge of the shoulder there were two trees and then a steep slope of broken ground.

The two cars behind stopped side by side 20 yards back from the Oldsmobile.

"Three people," said Colly. "One girl."

"More in front," said Jenny. "Bloody throngs. Two girls. Coed massacre. I don't know what to do."

Two men got out of the car in the road. One was burly; he looked like a college athlete, a letterman. The other was collegiate too, but not an athlete, a Phi Beta Kappa with a gun in his hand.

"No way out behind," said Colly. "They blocked the road with the cars."

"Same in front," said Jenny.

The athlete shut the driver's door of the car. He said something to the girl in the front of the car. The scholar joined him and they walked with guns in their hands towards the Oldsmobile.

Sandro said: *"Cretini.* Amateurs. There is a chance."

"Yes, darling," said Jenny softly. "Can you drive this?"

"Si. Autmoatic. My left foot. No problem."

Jenny put her gun in her lap. She said: "Start shooting, gents."

The men were 12 feet away and coming warily forward with raised guns.

Jenny put the car into drive and jumped on the accelerator. The big car plunged forward and hit the two men. They should have been well apart but they were together so Jenny could point the car at them both. They tried to jump out of the way, one to each side, but neither made it. The burlier man on the left was hit by the car's left headlamp as he jumped. He was hurled on to the ground by the car which then ran over his stomach. There was a big bump as the front wheel ran over him and then another bump as the back wheel went over him. He

123

screamed once, briefly, when he was hit by the car but he made no other sound. The scholarly man on the right was caught by the wing. Instead of being knocked down he was picked up by the car and carried. His head smashed down on to the hood of the car when he was picked up out of the road. He screamed then and continued to scream although there was not much left of his face.

Colly had smashed a hole in the rear window of the Oldsmobile with the muzzle of the gun as soon as the car began to move. He fired rapidly at the cars behind, more in order to keep their heads down and spoil their own aim than with much hope of hitting any of them. His own aim was spoiled by the bumps when the car went over the big man; two of his shots went wild.

Sandro in the front seat could not fire at the other cars because Jenny was in the way. She would not be there long and his pistol was ready.

Jenny stopped the Oldsmobile close behind the car which was parked in the road. The man on the hood was screaming out of the scarlet disintegration of his face.

Jenny got out of the Oldsmobile. A bullet chipped the road beside her and another clanged on the roof of the car. Relief flickered in her brain for a split second. She had not smashed her car into two innocent men carrying toy guns for a laugh. Running into people with a car was not pleasant but it was more pleasant then being murdered. The man on the hood was still screaming horribly but Jenny had to get on. Bent double she ran three yards to the car which blocked their way. To get in it and drive was the only way they could get out of this. If the man she ran over had taken the key out of the other car they were done.

A girl leaned out of the passenger seat of the car. She shot at Jenny. Jenny felt the sudden and shocking pain of a bullet in the left arm. She fired back at the girl and hit her full in the face. She was a better shot than the girl in the car. A hole appeared in the cheekbone under the girl's right eye and she was knocked backwards from the car's window.

Rapid fire from two guns came from the car on the shoulder. Jenny was in the cover of the car in the road. She sent two quick snap shots at the other car. Then, keeping low, she opened the door of her own new car. The dead girl lay in a puddle of blood across the bench front seat of

124

the car. Jenny climbed over her, fighting down nausea. There was no time to move the girl's body. Jenny fired two more shots at the car on her left. Sandro was also firing at this car.

The car started at once with the key. Jenny released the handbrake with her good arm. She thanked God for another car with automatic drive. The car's back wheels spun for a moment in the broken surface of the road, then bit. The car lurched forward. A bullet clanged somewhere on the metalwork and a window exploded; glass flew all over Jenny and over the dead girl beside her.

As soon as Jenny was out of the driving seat of the Oldsmobile Sandro slid along the seat and under the wheel. He was already firing out of the window as he moved, covering Jenny as she got into the cover of the car in front. Sandro hit his injured thigh on the steering wheel and the pain was bad for a moment. The man on the hood of the car was making a noise like a crazy bird, like an injured owl, an awful screech not in the voice of a man. Colly was firing out of the back of the car.

There were shots from directly in front: two, then two more. Sandro glanced ahead. Jenny was getting into the car. There was blood on the sleeve of her blue and white checked shirt. The noise of firing was almost continuous, three guns behind, two in front, Sandro's and Colly's and Jenny's guns. But all the people were protected by the heavy metal of expensive cars and it was possible that no one would get hit except by broken glass.

The car in front started moving. It skidded and then roared forwards. Sandro got the Oldsmobile moving. He kept as low as possible as they passed the car on the shoulder. A bullet smashed into the frame of the window by his head. The ricochets were dangerous and unpredictable. They were not hit. Sandro accelerated hard and they screamed round the next corner after Jenny. Colly put a fresh clip in the magazine of his automatic. He took a last shot out of the rear window.

Before they were out of sight of the other cars, Colly saw that the two behind them were moving.

Jenny saw in her rear mirror that Sandro was following her. So far so good. Her arm would keep for a little while. It was not losing much blood. Pretty soon it would need binding up. It would be nice to get rid of the body beside

125

her but that could wait too. Sandro would like to get rid of the man on the front of his car but that was one more thing that must wait, but not for long, because it would not do to be seen driving along with a screaming wreck of a man on the front of the car.

The best thing was to stop as soon as possible and ambush anybody who came after them. But to do that Colly and Sandro would have to get out of their car and find cover beside the road. It was not possible. Sandro could get along but not Colly. He was slow and he needed help. There was unlikely to be time to haul him behind a rock.

Or turn off the road. But there was no turning until the next town. What would be waiting for them in the next town? Jenny had a hole in her arm and a dead girl beside her. Sandro had his passenger.

Or block the road with one of the cars, leaving it locked, and go on in the other. But one car would not block the road. However it was placed it was not big enough. They needed two cars to block the road and in most places they would need three.

Jenny felt incapable of planning. She felt tired and ill and her arm was hurting. The dead girl's head nudged her knee.

Sandro blasted his horn behind her. Two shorts and a long. Stop. Jenny clamped on her brakes and halted the car. Sandro came up beside her. He stopped in the middle of the road.

The man on the front of the Oldsmobile had stopped screaming. He was dead.

Sandro opened the doors of both cars. He heaved Colly from the Oldsmobile into the back of the other car. Colly grunted with pain but said nothing. They had discussed this move as they drove and Colly was ready for it. Jenny saw that Colly had unwrapped a great length of bandage from his leg. Sandro hobbled to the gas tank cap on the back of the Oldsmobile. Jenny understood. She gritted her teeth and pulled the dead girl out of the car. With only one arm she could not get her into the other car. She pushed the body under the car with her foot. It was not a way to treat a dead opponent but this was no time for fuss.

Sandro took off the cap of the gas tank and fed the bandage into the tank. He began to pull it out again.

The cars behind them were coming. They went fast, then

126

much slower. They were being careful. They were making a mistake.

Sandro paid out the gasoline-soaked bandage as far up the road as it would go. Jenny drove the other car to the point where the bandage ended. She got out of the car.

She said: "Drive round the next bend and I'll follow you."

"No, *carina*. Into the car quick. You drive."

Jenny got back under the wheel of the car. Sandro sat in the open door on the other side. He had a gun in one hand and a cigarette lighter in the other.

The cars behind them nosed round a bend into view. They were close together. They had picked up two other men and another girl. There were six people in the two cars. They could not see Sandro's fuse running along the road. They could see three people in the car which had been Joe Steel's. They knew that there was no one waiting for them in the Olds. They had nothing to fear from the Olds.

Close together, one behind the other, they crept past the Olds in the small amount of road Sandro had left them.

Sandro lit the gas-soaked bandage with his lighter. He slammed his door and Jenny drove forward. The flame ran along the bandage to the gas tank of the Oldsmobile. There was a violent explosion in the gas tank. The car blew up. It knocked the leader of the two cars sideways. Burning gasoline and oil shrouded both cars. They were on fire. The people started to struggle out of the cars but they were too late. There were two more explosions, big bangs with brief incandescent blooms of pure light.

Jenny stopped the car at a safe distance. They looked back at the pyre.

"Now I look at that arm," said Sandro gently.

"All right," said Jenny. "But first I'm going to be sick."

"I've taken a dislike to petrol," said Jenny. "Quite turned against it."

"Saved our lives, baby."

"Yes. They don't have much luck with it, do they? Who *are* these people?"

Jenny was driving slowly between Anderson and Telfair, over the state line. She needed a doctor but not one so close to the bonfire on the mountain road. She and Sandro shared control of the car. Jenny operated the pedal and steered part of the time with her right hand. Sandro did some of the steering with his left hand and moved the lever of the automatic transmission the few times this was necessary. Colly said this arrangement was unsafe and illegal; he was right but they went slowly.

Jenny turned on the radio of the car at a moment when Sandro had the wheel. Instead of music there was a shrill electronic blip-blip in regular but complex rhythm.

"Trail-bug," said Colly immediately. "Signal from another car, I bet."

"Molto forte."

"Yes. How come? This noise isn't being made by a couple of transistors stuck under somebody's exhaust."

"From a car radio," said Sandro.

"Right. All the cars belonging to this outfit have them. This call is from the one we didn't burn. You know what we did? We underestimated this thing. We thought it was three or four blackmailers, but it's a goddam army. How the hell many more of these cars are we going to meet, full of college graduates with guns?"

Jenny said again: "Who *are* these people?"

She twiddled the knob of the radio and punched the buttons. It was not tuned to any commercial waveband. There were much fainter signals, perhaps the cars at a great distance. There was a high mosquito whine which seemed to come from a different type of transmitter.

"We need their code book to interpret this stuff," said Colly. "We ought to have searched that guy you squashed."

"No," said Jenny. "No no no."

The doctor in Telfair was competent and full of questions. He was told that Jenny's wound was an accident with a pistol. Sandro blamed himself to the doctor but Jenny said that it was her fault. Sandro and Jenny played crazy foreigners to the doctor. Colly said he would keep them out of further trouble, and not lend them any more pistols to shoot at bottles with.

Jenny's arm was cleaned out and dressed. It hurt a lot. There would be a scar and the bicep muscle was damaged. She said she had never had any biceps anyway.

"To cops or not to cops?" said Colly.

"Not," said Sandro. "It will start a nest egg."

"I doubt it," said Jenny.

"A mare's nest. We will have great troubles, long stories not believed by anybody, Mr. Cordle, Gabetti, truck salesmen and machinery brokers chasing their hats in the street. We know too much and not enough."

"This car we borrowed," said Jenny, "this elegant Pontiac. Its radio is going off blippety-blip to other ones, yes?"

"I guess so," said Colly. "And when we get south it's going to reach a hell of a long way."

"On account of being flat. No bumps."

"That's right."

"Fine. We'll tear the radio out by the roots."

"No, baby. For two reasons. One, there may be another trail-bug attached to the car, which we might have a hell of a job finding. Two, this is a stolen automobile. It belongs to a guy who doesn't exist, but—"

"Then he can't report it."

"His boss can. Anonymously. Then if a cop takes the number we're in all kinds of trouble."

"What we do," said Sandro, "is leave the car. It can signal to the friends of our friends. They come and find an empty car, nothing."

"They find two empty cars," said Jenny. "They left that other on the side of the road because it was pointing the wrong way to chase us."

"*Giusto.*"

"And what are people going to make of our little holocaust?" asked Colly.

"There is nothing to make. *Niente.* A man is run over and killed—"

"Ugh," said Jenny.

"Who has no identification, a non-man, a person who does not exist, like the two men in Gabetti's factory. Somewhere they have homes, mothers, dogs, names and numbers like other people, but when they come out in their cars to kill us they leave all that behind, yes? It is very clever of them. It is not an easy thing and they do it very well. So now. A little way along the road are three cars and many people. The people are beyond recognition. But they cannot be identified even if they are more complete because they are all non-people who do not exist. A man is

129

Mr. Harry Smith of Chicago. A girl is Miss Mary Jones of Los Angeles, *e tutto.*"

"The girls are a creepy aspect," said Jenny.

"Look who's talking," said Colly. "The hand that rocks the cradle pulls the goddam trigger."

"The cars can be identified," said Jenny.

"*Si,* by the number of the chassis, that is so. But they are owned by false men."

"We had some stuff in the Olds," said Colly. "But all anonymous and all burned up anyway."

"I think."

"Then we're clean?" said Jenny.

"With a new car we are clean. We go a little further away, get a new car, and make a plan."

"Yeah, we want one of those," said Colly. "Every home should have one."

Jenny drove, without too much discomfort, 30 miles to a much bigger town. Colly bought a good used car, a serviceable Ford. They left the Pontiac, its seat pretty clean of blood, in a crowded lot behind a moviehouse.

Jenny washed the blood off the sleeve of her blue and white checked shirt. She darned the bullet hole. It was her lucky shirt. She had twice escaped death when she was wearing it.

"I want to go home," said Colly. "I want to rest up in my apartment in New York. I want a steak dinner and play my hi-fi."

"Your apartment is watched and probably bugged," said Sandro. "If you go anywhere near it they will kill you. They must. We do not know why, but to them it is a necessary thing."

"Seems so. I have to admit the logic of that. I don't want to but I have to. We know something we don't know we know. Let us for Christ's sake get to know whatever it is we know, so we can do something about it."

"Always before," said Jenny, "when anybody was chasing us, we've known who it was and why. Such a comfort. It makes it easier to run away. Which is what I personally feel like doing."

"For ever?" asked Sandro.

"Yes. No. All right, fatty, get on with making your plans."

130

Jenny's blue and white shirt was dry. She put it on. Within a few minutes her body heat activated the pinhead minisqueep hidden in the stitching of the shoulder. It began to broadcast its high, mosquito-whine oscillating signal.

CHAPTER ELEVEN

They continued southwest. After 100 miles, which was far enough for Sandro and much too far for Jenny, they stopped. They rested for two days in a small place near Hazard. They did not like staying in one place for so long but it was necessary for them all.

"Bugs," said Colly. "Bugs every place. Grab that and a lot of things come clear."

"Not to me," said Jenny.

"They do too, you stupid limey cow. For intance, how did those two guys know you and Sandro were in Gabetti's office that night? We thought and we thought, and we couldn't make out how they knew to come around. Now it's obvious."

"Ah."

"They bugged his office when they did their deal with him."

"Not very trusting."

"There's a lot of that about. Then again, how did the guy with the pump know we were at Lake Dodge?"

"They bugged the cabin? How could they, when they didn't know—"

"Stupid, stupid, they bugged my car."

"Oh I see. Yes, I might have thought of that. All right, clever. So they knew Gabetti did those deals, or started them, because his office was bugged, they heard him talking about them, yes. So they killed the people who knew Gabetti had money. Why did they?"

"I guess Gabetti was jumping the gun. Throwing the money around too soon. It's how a hell of a lot of crimes come unstuck. These boys were too careful to permit that."

"Yes, I suppose so. That must be it. But how? How did they do those murders? Did they bug the motorbike? Did they bug that poor man's hat to make it blow off in the street?"

"These people," rumbled Sandro, whom the others had believed asleep, "are blackmailers using the technology of modern espionage.

"Very neatly put, chum. I couldn't have expressed it better myself."

"I couldn't have expressed it at all," said Jenny.

"They are many. They have good organization and discipline. They have expensive electronics. All those things make them very hard to find. But they cannot be hidden all the time, like a little gang of thieves. They cannot stay in the sewers. They must buy cars and radios, they must go about in the daylight in nice clothes."

"In fact they must have a pretty good cover," said Colly.

"What cover?" asked Jenny.

"Private detective agency. But that would be risky. One-man outfits in back streets can play dice with the law if they want, but not the big firms. They keep their noses terribly clean."

"What, then?" asked Jenny.

"Baby, I truly don't know. Maybe a department of an ad agency, they're always snooping at each other. Maybe guys on a newspaper—undercover reporting with this on the side."

"You just don't know, do you?"

"That's what I've been trying to tell you."

"Then, obviously," said Jenny, "it's perfectly clear what we have to do."

"Bene," said Sandro dryly. But he listened with attention.

Jenny pushed back her bright gold hair with her good hand. She turned her breathtaking pink-gold face towards Sandro, and opened wide her miraculously silly eyes. The signs of strain and pain in her face would not have been visible to a stranger but they were visible to Sandro.

"We must have a company," said Jenny. "One of Colly's might do, I'm sorry to have to admit. It must have a secret
133

new invention. Somebody must get drunk and babble a bit about this invention. The news must get to a rival company, a competitor, a stinky nasty-minded lot. They'll try and find out about the invention by themselves, and fail. So then they'll whistle up your espionage people."

"No, *cara*. We maybe meet the spy this way, but he is the wrong one, he never heard of blackmail or of us."

"Hold it," said Colly, "hold it. Somebody was spying on Dave Cordle. Somebody wanted to know what gave in the Cordle office, and they hired an eye to find out. What he found out about the office God knows, but he found out something about Dave."

"Ha," said Sandro. "We have maybe found the way to begin."

"Of course I remember you, Mr. Tucker," said Gloria Baynes from the office at Spruce Ledge. "I was horrified to hear about your crash."

She said she was still working there and would continue in the service of the companies. She had been promoted owing to her close knowledge of the business; she was no longer a secretary but an officer of the company.

"Well now, Miss Baynes," said Colly, talking in an hotel room in Chattanooga, "this is going to sound weird."

He asked her if there had been any secret operations going on in the office, there in Vermont, not in New York, which an outsider could profit, really profit, from knowing about.

"I don't want to know what the secret is," said Colly. "I just want to know if there was one."

"Thirty," said Miss Baynes at once. "What I have in mind is investment decisions, our diversification. Like a lot of companies we have been hedging our bets, so to speak, spreading the load like an investment portfolio. Your own companies have been doing much the same, as you know."

"Why, ah, sure," said Colly heartily.

"When we buy a company, or a major share in the equity of a company, it does a few dramatic things to stock market quotations."

"That I follow."

"An unprincipled outsider could make a great deal of money anticipating our movements."

"I still follow. Did anybody do that?"

"Not that I know of."

"Did you have any snoopers up there?"

"Again, not that I know of. But if they were good snoopers I suppose none of us would know. It's not exactly a fortress."

"Thank you, Miss Baynes. I'm really grateful."

"You're very welcome, Mr. Tucker. I wish I could be more help in whatever it is you're doing."

"She gave me a sense of direction," said Colly, "but nothing firm. But say Cordle decides there's a big future in, ah, photograph frames."

"Gracious, is there? I've got hundreds."

"Several types of people can make money out of knowing this decision in advance, but the guy who can make most out of it is a gent who already makes photograph frames."

"I don't want to meet him," said Jenny. "He's not getting my custom."

"*Al telephono di nuovo, povere,*" said Sandro.

Colly telephoned a brokerage house on Wall Street. Later in the same day he was given, on the telephone in his hotel room, a list of five industries in which the Cordle group had invested more or less heavily in recent months. These were: packaging, travel and tourism, cassette movies, aerosols, and educational books.

The packaging company had been owned by descendants of its founders. The shares were independently valued. No profit could have been made by anticipating Cordle's plans.

The travel company was set up in collaboration with a national magazine. Shares were exchanged between the two groups. It was a large and complicated piece of brokerage, widely publicized. Cordle's intentions were known throughout the travel business long before anything was finalized.

The cassette movie affair was a flotation. Cordle offered the public 35% of the equity with all the financial publicity that affects such operations. Profits were made by initial subscribers to the issue who sold out quickly, but they were modest profits made legitimately and in public.

This left aerosols and educational books. Take-overs were involved in both cases, with rocketing share values.

"We're guessing like crazy mad," said Colly, "but since we're having fun let's go right on doing it. Aerosols. I don't

135

know a goddam thing about aerosols."

"Don't you?" said Jenny. "Well, what you do with an aerosol is press the tit at the top, and—"

"I don't believe we have a finger in that pie."

"If you did," said Jenny, "you'd never get it out."

"But educational publishing, it just so happens, we do have a finger in. Both hands, in fact. Three imprints last time I heard. Morning Glory Books for Beginners. Dick and Pat see the cow. Do you see the cow? And then there's the Let's Make Whoozis Fun series."

"Can it be fun?" asked Jenny, "ever?"

"Let's Make Algebra Fun. Let's Make Spelling Fun. Let's Make—"

"Okay, belt up, I'm with you."

"And Great Stories Retold For Small People."

"Ick."

"Pretty ick, I admit."

"*Les Miserables* for the rompers set."

"I wonder if they thought of that one? You might like to be one of our assistant editors, darling. Tackle de Sade and *Lady Chatterley*. Of course we don't pay much, but the *real* reward—"

"Morning Glory Books must fly a kite."

"A kite. Yeah. Morning Glory Books. I don't see it yet. It didn't hit me."

"Something that's going to make the competition want like hell to know what you've got."

"Let's Make Sadism Fun. Kids are so advanced nowadays, darling, I doubt if we can shock anybody . . . No, it suddenly did hit me. This isn't an editorial thing at all. It's something to do with production or distribution. A way to make a great big beautiful durable kid-proof book, or a way to crash the whole goddam list into every grade school in the U.S.A. . . . No no, you'd have to do that by bribery, it has to be production. Plastic books. Polythene bonded on to paper so you can scribble all you want and wipe them clean with a rag—"

"Drip Dry Books."

"I believe we have it. I believe we do."

The leaks were carefully managed and timed. There were several leaks. A young salesman got overexcited in a bar in Des Moines with a gabby librarian and two rival salesmen. A senior editor's asides to a colleague were overheard at a convention of specialized publishers. A federal agency reported nontoxicity of a paper-like plastic material and its inks, another government laboratory confirmed absolute fireproofness. A famous book designer let it drop to a reporter that he had been approached on a secret project that enchanted him, quite enchanted him, children being his delight, his greatest delight, but he mustn't say another word . . .

Cold, greedy brains collated these snippets. The material and the way it was printed and bound had been developed abroad and were protected by a foreign patent. The sheets were a matt white unless colored, and handled like stiff paper. The material could not be crumpled or torn. Its edges did not cut. It would take halftone illustrations as well as line blocks and the range of colors was infinite. There was no fading or deterioration of any kind. "Paper" and inks were harmless and fireproof; the stuff could be chewed by a baby and you could put a match to it. You could write on it with an ordinary pen, ballpoint, felt tip, crayon or pencil; it could be wiped clean with a damp cloth; generations of children could do their sums in the same books . . .

Essentially the material was understood to be a polyethylene. But there was something extremely special about the process of its manufacture, a question of temperature when it was rolled, cut, and immediately printed and bound. Rumors of the critical temperature varied widely; some said that the stuff had to be freezing, some said at boiling point.

The price was the most remarkable thing. Provided the runs were large and before the cost of distribution and of wholesalers' and bookstores' markups, manufacture was so simple that each book costed out at a few cents a copy.

Laboratories threw themselves into imitating the new material, which, under pressure, Tucker Publishing admitted existed. They said it was called L.G.3 and refused to answer questions about it. None of the laboratories came up with anything to touch L.G.3.

It was said that Drip Dry Books (their nickname throughout publishing) would be manufactured in Mexico owing to supplies of raw materials.

"I like this place," said Jenny. "But we've been here an

137

awful long time."

She sat with Sandro outside a cafe in the plaza in the early evening. The plaza looked like the hub of a big and rich town with booming local industries, the center of a lush farming area, the railhead for mines of precious metals. But the town was small and poor. It had no local industry. Tillage of the nearby countryside was by burro and wooden plough; there were lean goats, few cows, and no horses. The nearest railroad was at Uruapan, not far but further than anybody went. There was, should anyone require it, a good road to Uruapan.

The plaza had an Opera House crowned with allegorical statuary; lurid posters on its ornate portico announced the movies showing or expected. There was a Cathedral, soaring baroque, with earth-shaking bells and the relics of an uncanonical local saint. There was a bandstand like the paper frill round a Christmas cake; on Sunday evenings men in uniform, but barefooted, played a small repertoire of tunes on big brass instruments. There was the Hotel Villanazul, in need of paint. There were several cafes with awnings and cracked adobe walls. Off the plaza ran small, steep alleys, cobbled, with reeking gutters. Outside the *carnecerias* in the alleys hung the carcasses of animals; to inspect the meat you had to hit it with a stick to drive away the flies which covered it. The houses were tiny and jumbled together. The few larger buildings held many families. The people were dark-skinned, with Indian features. Their Spanish took some getting used to. Much of the imagery of their fiestas was derived from sources remote from Christianity. They were a dignified people, unhurried, quiet-voiced except when celebrating, decorous except when drunk, perfect mannered except when angry. There were few pure-bred Spaniards and fewer gringos.

The climate in these highlands was hot and very dry by day, often cold at night; but where the Tepalcatepec flowed into the Rio de las Balsas there was tropical rainforest, bottomless and snake-filled jungle, for all the 100 miles to the Pacific. It was this combination which, among less obvious advantages, brought the team of men in crumpled suits in their big cars to the province of Michoacan. They said that they were also attracted by the unlimited hydroelectric power of the big mountains and fast rivers. Security, they explained to officials in Morelia and Palzcuaro, led them to look for somewhere remote. A big, disused police barracks, relic of a local war lord, brought them to this town, as well as the chemical composition of certain springs up hill to the southwest.

The crumpled men spoke for long hours to the *alcalde* and other dignitaries in their offices and in the cafes of the plaza. They revealed themselves as men of books, which had the awesomeness of the unusual in the town. Their pockets were full of dollars. Though red of face, they were polite and respectful men. They did business at a seemly tempo. They were not like the hectic, uncaring tourists, of whom the town saw few, milked as hard as possible, and ejected with relief; nor like the impatient hustlers from the big American oil companies and soft drink companies; nor at all like the pale-eyed heretics from Lutheran or Methodist missions.

The police barracks lay outside the town, beyond the palatial cemetery. The buildings had fat adobe walls and roofs of pink tiles. The farmers and families who had used them were generously compensated. Jobs were offered and reluctantly taken, the buildings were cleaned out, holes in the roofs mended, and concrete slabs laid in the ground.

Machines in crates came by the railroad to Uruapan and then to the town by truck. The machinery was less, in bulk and weight, then might have been supposed. It was not, however, complete. It was bolted to the slabs of concrete in the grateful shade of the police barracks. The people of the town came to look at it. They were not to touch it, but the hot and crumpled Americans had no objection to anyone looking at it, not now that it was still incomplete. The Americans welcomed visitors, saying that they were the guests of the town and that they would try to repay courtesy with courtesy.

"Senor," said the *alcalde* one evening to the most important of the crumpled men (he with the reddest face and the wettest armpits), "although we are glad that you are here we do not understand it. We do not wish to pry but curiosity is natural."

"We have explained," said the American in his careful schoolboy Spanish. "Your humidity—"

"Yes, you have explained that you like our climate here, our water, the electricity, the road, the barracks. We understand also that you give our people smaller wages than

139

your own people would demand, for reasons which we all comprehend."

Flustered, the American said: "If you think we're being stingy, why—"

The *alcalde* held up a hand, at once to silence his companion and to call a waiter. "You are not stingy. Your wages are more than fair. The men are happy with them. They will not ask for more in case you become angry and go away. It is still mysterious to us, who have discussed the matter at great length and on many occasions, why you put a factory *here*."

The American glanced to right and to left. At a table to the right, well out of earshot, sat a priest, the good Padre Tomas. At a table to the left sat the Italian writer, the big archaeologist; beyond him was his secretary, the crazy blonde British girl. The Italian's colleague, the American cartographer from Oxford, was not with them. Probably he was drawing his maps, or developing pictures in the cellars of the Hotel Villanazul.

"Senor Gutierrez," said the American solemnly, "if a man, a foreigner, was to come here, how many people would know about it how soon?"

"The whole town. 3000 people. In one minute."

"Yes. And if I say to you and to the people of the town: it is important that no stranger, no scientist who understands machinery, gets into the police barracks, then how many strangers will get into the barracks?"

"None."

"That is your answer. It must sound strange to you—"

"A little. I had not thought that printing books was such a secret affair."

"Nor had I. Nor was it. But this is a new kind of book, made in a way that I do not myself understand. That is the reason for my orders."

"From the Senor Tucker?"

"I suppose so. Not directly, you understand."

"Do you know Senor Tucker?"

"I met one, Franklyn Tucker, a very careful man."

"So it appears."

Sandro and Jenny heard this conversation, though neither seemed to be listening or interested.

Jenny murmured: "He's right. Whoever peeps at those

machines when we get started is going to have to be good at it."

"Yes, the best, the most expensive."

"Have we made this too difficult?"

"If we were spies, *cara*, we could look at these machines."

"Now, yes."

"Now and later."

A swarthy magazine salesman from Mexico City came to the town in a dusty Chevrolet. He unpacked a case and visited each *farmicia botica*, all the drugstores that sold magazines and books. He showed them his firm's publications; the covers were pictures of bullfights and of movie stars. He did a little business, heard a lot of gossip, wandered up to the police-barracks to inspect the town's new marvel, and after three days went quietly away again.

He reported in code by Telex to New York. He described the machinery accurately. He said that its control mechanisms were not yet installed. Until this happened all the difficult questions about the process remained unanswerable. When the control mechanisms arrived the security would be quite a different thing. Tight security would be simple to impose on the police barracks. Intelligence would be tough to get. It would not be impossible but it would be difficult and expensive.

More crates arrived. They were unpacked with care. Visitors were no longer allowed to the police barracks. In this the Americans had the full cooperation of the *alcalde* and police of the town.

A *farmaceutico* sent a card by the post to Mexico City. He had been bought many mugs of beer by the magazine salesman. His card apparently conveyed a message of fulsome good wishes; it conveyed to his generous friend that the control mechanisms had arrived.

Another Telex went to New York.

On a shelf in Jenny's room at the Hotel Villanazul lay her blue and white checked shirt. She wore it sometimes. She remained fond of it. When she had worn it for a short time, the tiny transmitter in the stitching of the shoulder emitted a high, oscillating signal on ultra short wave.

141

CHAPTER TWELVE

Superficially Jenny's wound was healing nicely, but her arm was not much good.

Sandro walked fairly well with a stick, less well without one. He could not hurry. The muscles of his thigh had a long way to go before he was fully fit again.

Colly had been X-rayed in San Antonio. His two compound fractures still needed time. He was still in plaster.

They lived in comfort at the Hotel Villanazul. Miss Norrington from Yorkshire, Signor Ganzarello from Torino, and Dick Coleridge, once of Harvard but now holder of a lectureship at the University of Reading, England. Their stories were believed and their presence gave general satisfaction. The people of the town knew that they came from a proud and ancient race beside whom the gringos and Spaniards were uncouth upstarts; it was most proper that their antiquity should be studied. The archaeologists were familiar and respected figures in the town before the hot, crumpled men first arrived from Tucker Publishing. Sandro was *muy hombre,* and Jenny a *senorita dorada.*

The new American arrivals were at first surprised at the exotic trio they found in residence in the town. But by now nobody else was surprised, so the newcomers became accustomed to the three; they were part of the scenery of the town and of the plaza cafes in the evening.

One of the Americans thought he had seen Sandro. Sandro explained that he had once been, with an interpreter, on a television talk-show in New York. None of the

Americans had seen Colly or Jenny before. Colly had never seen any of these employees of his family's corporation.

Jenny talked to the Chief of Police of the town on their first coming. She told him a story that horrified him. She was pursued by a rich and cruel man who wanted her for a plaything. The Chief of Police had heard of such men. He knew something of the world although he lived in a small, poor town in a remote part of Mexico. He had seen a movie at the Opera House in which Edward G. Robinson played such a man. Not a new film but, in the estimation of the Chief of Police, a masterpiece of the cinema. The rich and cruel man who pursued the senorita sounded much like the one played by Edward G. Robinson. He had a great many minions, some of whom were back street cutthroats but some could be made to seem respectable. He had sent his minions after Jenny but so far she had escaped them. The very thought of the rich cruel man and his minions made Jenny tremble. She broke down in the cool, cigar-scented office of the Chief of Police. He comforted her as best he could, reminding himself sternly that he was a figure of importance in the community and father of an immense family. He promised that no stranger would come within miles of the town without Jenny and her friends being told.

Strangers came: the men from Tucker Publishing, men of business of various kinds and colorings. Jenny trembled at each strange face, and trotted to the office of the Chief of Police. Always he reassured her. The men were known to him, or had impeccable credentials; the very few tourists had their papers scrutinized and their baggage covertly searched. None were the emissaries of the man who so terrified the senorita, the animal whom, by Jesus on earth, the Chief of Police would dearly like to meet . . .

More crates arrived from the railroad at Uruapan. The crumpled Americans no longer welcomed visitors at the old police barracks.

The Chief of Police swore once again to Jenny that any stranger for whom he could not entirely vouch would be reported to her at once. He said the same, on behalf of the *alcalde* of the town, to the American gentlemen from Tucker Publishing.

143

It was a cool evening after a day of baking dry heat. The plaza was crowded but not noisy.

Jenny sat with Sandro and Colly at a table on the tiled patio of the Cafe Tacambaro. They drank wine. It was pleasant. Acquaintances who passed their table greeted them with grave courtesy. The waiter Luis, whose face was carved out of lava rock, came and stood by the table when his duties permitted. He asked respectfully after the progress of their studies. He liked to think that his own Indian ancestors had built fortresses, palaces and tombs until they were destroyed by his other, Spanish, ancestors. Jenny and Colly replied in correct Castilian Spanish which was strange to Luis's ears.

A policeman, very smart and official in his buttoned uniform, craved a confidential word. Luis took a step to the rear; if he felt curiosity his rock-like face betrayed none. He bowed himself away from the table. He went to inspect the tortillas frying indoors, the flat maize cakes which accompanied drinks. Their pungent frying smell filled the quiet air in front of the cafe, arousing both hunger and thirst. There was no need for Luis to inspect the tortillas. They were more than adequately supervised by Filomena and by her daughter Ramona, who was the prettiest girl in the town. But it was more *cortes*, more tactful and correct, for an errand to take him away than for him simply to depart because another had arrived. The policeman Esteban was a friend of Luis. It would not do for Esteban to think that he had driven Luis away. So Luis went to frown at the frying tortillas with Filomena and the very beautiful Ramona.

Esteban sat down at the table. He accepted a glass of wine. He said that strangers had come to the town. Jenny betrayed agitation. Esteban came near to patting her hand. No harm would come to her. She was assured of the protection of the law.

The strangers were *geologos*. Was the senorita familiar with the word? Esteban admitted that he had himself only just learned its meaning. The men were students of rocks. By examining rocks, it appeared that they could tell what happened when God created the mountains and valleys. They could tell if there were valuable minerals in the rocks or below them: gold and silver, turquoise or mica, coal or oil. What a wonderful thing it would be for the town if any

144

of these things were found by the gentlemen. They had little hammers with which to strike at the rocks; Esteban had
seen the hammers, from which they were never parted.
They had also instruments for measuring, tools for boring
holes, and cases for specimens.

There were two of these men. They were American.
They came from California, from Los Angeles, a city with
a fine name although American. They were staying not at
the Hotel Villanazul but at the even less expensive Hotel
Comercial. An opportunity would speedily be found for
their rooms and baggage to be searched. The search would
be *lleno de tacto,* in keeping with the good manners of the
town; the men would not notice or become angry. Esteban
was certain that the men were what they seemed; meanwhile the senorita was as safe as the Infant Jesus in his
crib.

Esteban went away to give the same message, with the
same assurances, to the Americans of the book printing,
who sat at a table outside the Cafe de los Santos.

"Tools and instruments," said Colly. "By the pricking of
my thumbs something creepy this way comes."

Ed Burns went back to his room at the Hotel Comercial
to freshen up for dinner. It was a crummy room but he did
not expect to be in it for long.

He had left the room tidy and it was still tidy. He looked
for a piece of thread which he had left over the keyhole of
the one drawer which could be locked. The thread had
gone. The things inside the drawer were tidy: too tidy: he
had left one piece of paper at an angle with the other
papers and now it was perfectly aligned with them.

Someone had searched the room thoroughly and
carefully.

Who? Why? Another outfit on the same assignment?

There was a knock on Ed's door. Ty Matheson came in
fuming.

"Did somebody search your room?" said Ty.

"Yeah."

"What the hell?"

"I don't know what the hell."

They accosted Senor Reyes, the manager of the hotel.
He was deeply shocked. He knew nothing about any
search. Was anything missing? Had they anything secret in

145

their rooms? Were the rooms left dirty or in confusion? Well then, although an outrageous liberty had without doubt been taken, no harm was done.

"That bastard," said Ty later in Ed's room, "was lying in his teeth."

"Maybe."

"I'd like to hitch him to an electroencephalograph and ask him again."

"Okay, he's lying. But I don't know how you can be sure. These people have faces like copper masks, like zombies. Either way we have to get on with the job."

"I'd like to know who did it. Who hired them and for what. How they rumbled us."

"Did they rumble us? How could they? Look, Ty, we have to get on with this job and do it quick. If anybody's snooping at us we'll probably spot them."

"I say find out who's snooping, get them off our backs, and then get on with the job."

"No time. We'll do it my way."

Ty grumbled. But Ed was in charge and they would do it his way.

"Something called postgraduate geologists," said Jenny, "from something called U.C.L.A., being sponsored by something called the Nevada Mineral Something Inc."

"Yes?" said Colly.

"Yes. And everything they've got belongs to geology or Los Angeles or both. One of them brought his diary and address book along—"

"Why would he do that?"

"So, he's got the addresses to send all his postcards to, stupid. I'd do it myself if I ever had an address book, and if I ever wanted to send any postcards. This man has friends in San Diego and Monterey and so on, but not a single one outside the state of California. Is that possible?"

"Perfectly possible," said Colly. "Californians don't bother with the rest of the Union. They don't have to. They don't even want to."

"There you are, then."

"Where, baby?"

"With a man whose cover is too good to be true. And the dates he had, according to his diary—"

"You read his diary? Mind-blowing stuff, I guess,

146

knowing those wild young geologists at U.C.L.A."

"Engagement book, not record of seductions or religious experiences. All his dates were in greater Los Angeles."

"Naturally. It takes a day to cross the area."

"The other bloke has a bunch of letters from a girl."

"Did you read his *letters?*"

"Called Marcia."

"That figures."

"Addressed to somewhere in Westwood."

"Also figures. Near the college."

"He's got a photograph of Marcia. At least I trust it's Marcia."

"Pretty girl?"

"She fits with a postgraduate geologist. So does every other bloody thing about both of them. Clothes, books, kit, papers, letters, everything. They've got nothing the slightest bit surprising, nothing out of character."

"Then I guess my thumb pricks gave me a bum steer."

"No," said Jenny. "Everybody has things out of character. Every pack has a joker. A character wouldn't be a character, not a real one, unless it had things out of it."

"Go gentle, baby. Take that bar again at half speed."

"People are inconsiderate."

"Some yes, some no. Take my own case—"

"I mean inconsistent. For instance, since you mentioned your case, some years ago I remember seeing you reading a book."

"Only a page," said Colly. "Then I ran out of gas. I had to go lie down for an hour."

"These men," said Sandro unexpectedly to Jenny, "are phoney because they are too perfect?"

"Barmy as it sounds," said Jenny, "I think they might be. I think a man brings an address book here, with nothing but Californian addresses, because he actually comes from Jersey City. So we'll have to wait and see if they kill us. Ramona will be *very* sorry if they kill you, fatty."

"That is true," said Sandro.

Ed Burns and Ty Matheson started work first thing in the morning, wearing Panama hats from California, and California shirts, pants and shoes. They were observed all day as they inspected the hillside above the town. They were in full view of the old police barracks but they were

147

several hundred yards away from it. They were watched through binoculars from a window in the barracks. They were watched by an impassive goatherd, further up the dry white hill, who was earning a few pesos from the Chief of Police. They were watched, though not continuously, by Sandro and Jenny.

They tapped rocks with their hammers. They collected chips of rocks in boxes. They made holes in rocks with drills. They peered through instruments. They took photographs. They never peered in the direction of the police barracks. The photographs they took were of rock formations far from the police barracks.

They went back to the Hotel Comercial burdened with rock samples.

"There," said Colly smugly. "Because a guy's address book is full of California addresses you have to assume he isn't a Californian. Going along from there you assume he isn't a geologist. Screwiest reasoning I ever heard in my life. What in hell did they act like today?"

"Act is right," said Jenny. "Acting is what they were doing. At least I think so."

"So will you watch as hard tomorrow and the next day and the day after that? Will the boys in the printing press or barracks or whatever we call it now? Will the police?"

"Yes," said Jenny.

"You're nuts."

"No good," said Ed Burns, looking at the still-wet prints through a magnifying glass.

"There's something there."

"We knew that before we started. That's why we're here."

Ed's tripod mounted camera had a long handgrip at the side. It was unusually fat but not otherwise remarkable. It ended in a plastic knob which could be removed with a twist of finger and thumb. It contained a telephoto lens of immense power. A prismatic mirror inside the camera meant that both lens and viewfinder pointed at 90 degrees from the apparent direction of the photograph. Normal photographs of the rock formations on the hillside turned out to be much enlarged shots through the windows of the police barracks.

But Ed was right. They were not good enough. There

148

was unfamiliar control mechanism on the machinery: quite unfamiliar: weird. So much was obvious. So much had been predicted. But the men inside the building had hung screens over the windows. The screens blurred the pictures. It was impossible to extrapolate the technology of the control mechanism from its general outline or the few details identifiable.

"We have to go closer."

"Yeah."

Getting closer was no problem. They were looking at right angles to the photographs they were taking. They were still a good way away.

They developed the results in Ed's hotel room the next evening and it was still no good.

They went closer still the third day. Shutters had been put over the windows of the police barracks.

Ty was at boiling point and Ed was not too pleased himself.

That night they tried to get into the place. They had to try. They stumbled on a piece of electric fencing which gave Ty a jolt in the leg; then a trip-wire which started an alarm bell. Lights came on and people started shouting. They beat it back to the town and a bar just off the plaza.

The following evening, at the hour when the town took drinks in the plaza, they bugged the bedrooms of the Tucker men in the Hotel Villanazul. The bugs were only a half-inch across and deep, easily concealed, short-range but powerful enough to reach from hotel to hotel. The wire recorders in the bottoms of the specimen cases were to run all the time the Tucker men were in their hotel rooms.

Ed plugged a lead into his normal-looking transistor radio. The other end would go to the recorder when the radio was tuned. He began to tune the radio to the U.S.W. frequency of the first bug.

He took the radio out on to the balcony of his room. Thirty yards away he could see the lights of the Hotel Villanazul. Low rooftops and a few chimneys lay between, and a cobbled alley full of flies, sewage and the evening smell of fried tortillas.

Delicately Ed turned the tuning-knob towards the frequency of the first bug. To his great surprise, on a different but nearby frequency, he got a completely different signal: a high oscillating whine.

"Hey, Ty, listen to this."

Ty came out on to the balcony.

He listened a moment. He said: "Very small, very close. I only heard that once before but I recognize it."

"Yeah?"

"The U.S. Army developed them. Used in Viet Nam. You scatter them out of an airplane. They stick to uniforms, vehicles, guys' hair, anything. They respond to vibration, body temperature, body odor. There are various types activated by various stimuli. Normally you feed the signal straight into a computer. The computer tells you a brigade of troops is moving one way or 30 trucks are moving another way."

"What the hell is a bug like that doing in a place like this?"

"I think we should find out before we do anything else. I know you're in charge, Ed, but—"

"This time I agree. Can we get a direction-fix?"

"Sure, with the other radio."

Ty tuned the U.S.W. band of his radio to the same frequency. He took it to the balcony of his own room. The strength of the signal varied according to the angle of the radios. They could draw imaginery lines from both radios in the direction of the source. The source was where the lines intersected.

As they expected, the intersection was the Hotel Villanazul. Somebody in the hotel had picked up a minute electronic bug.

The signal faded. Ty rejoined Ed.

"Gone to have a drink."

"Let's get to the square," said Ed.

"With the radios?"

"Why not? Everybody carries radios. They can't stand to stop listening to *La Paloma*."

They went down into the plaza. The signal returned, strong, oscillating, a high insect whine. They turned down the volume on both radios so that the signal would not be noticed by people in the plaza. They separated. Ed started down the north side of the plaza by the Cathedral, Ty down the west side by the Opera House. They were sauntering casually, busy men relaxing in the evening, enjoying the sights and sounds and smells of the plaza like the people of the town.

"There's a Californian geologist," said Jenny, "listening to his radio. He ought to wait for the band on Sunday."

"Ecco l'altro," said Sandro. "He likes music too."

Jenny was wearing her blue and white checked cotton shirt, her lucky shirt with the neat darn in the left sleeve.

CHAPTER THIRTEEN

Ed and Ty met round the corner from the Cafe Tacambaro.

"One of those three," said Ty. "The archaeologists. Wop, American, limey girl."

"Can we tell which?"

"Not without joining them at their table. Not until they split up."

"If they don't split up?"

"They must go to the can sometimes."

Ed and Ty sat at a table in front of the next cafe. They sat for some time, drinking little, their radios innocently on the table between them, innocently turned towards the table at the Cafe Tacambaro.

The big wop got up. He limped into the cafe. He could be seen sampling a tortilla given him by the dimpling Ramona under the basilisk eye of her mother Filomena.

There was no change in the signal on the radios.

"American," said Ty.

"Or the girl."

"No way. How would a British chick come by something like that?"

The girl got up. She walked away from the Cafe Tacambaro. Ed and Ty both noticed how beautifully she moved, and how beautiful her figure was under the thin cotton clothes she wore. She walked 20 yards to another cafe where the Chief of Police was enjoying a drink with the *alcalde*. There was an enthusiastic reunion, although she saw the Chief of Police almost every day.

The signal faded, slightly but perceptibly, as she increased her distance from the radios.

"She's it," said Ty. "I don't get it. Who dropped a bug on her out of an airplane in Viet Nam?"

"Nobody, for Christ's sake."

"Of course not. But how does she come to be toting round a piece of top-secret U.S. Government electronics?"

"We have to find that out."

"Do we ask her?"

"In a manner of speaking," said Ed, "we ask her."

Jenny and Sandro helped Colly to bed. He was tired. His plaster casts were irksome in the tremendous heat of the daytime.

Sandro went to his room and Jenny to hers. Jenny's room was isolated from the other two bedrooms on the second floor of the Hotel Villanazul. The other two shared a bath and a balcony. Jenny had her own.

Jenny waved goodnight along the passage to Sandro. He waved back and disappeared into his room. She unlocked her door and opened it. She went into the room. She was tired herself. The room was in pitch darkness. The chambermaid Soledad had closed the shutters and windows and drawn the curtains; complaint, cajolery, bribery, threats did not deter Soledad from this routine. She had a clear idea of her duties. When the guests of the hotel were dining she made ready their bedrooms for the night; she turned down the beds, and closed the shutters and windows against the evil vapors of the night air, and drew the curtains against ghouls and peepers. So Jenny's room was pitch-dark, silent, rather stuffy. There was a faint smell of Jenny's own cigarettes, and of her scent and soap and talc.

Jenny felt a familiar prickle in the small of her back. She was alert and alarmed. As too often before in recent weeks she sensed something wrong, something foreign: as in Gabetti's flyblown shack in the shuddering dawn, as on the banks of the trout pond in the soft New England night, as on the empty little road in the West Virginia mountains.

There was somebody in the room. Somebody was waiting for her. Nothing gave this away except Jenny's awareness that it was so.

She began to back out of the room into the passage but

153

the door was closed behind her. The light came on. She heard the bolt of the door.

One of the Californian geologists was sitting on her bed with a gun in his lap. He looked ill at ease. The other came round from behind her, grinning with a mixture of triumph and apology.

Jenny thought: these people are soft.

At the same time they were in her room with guns. Her room was isolated. They could fire a shot and get clear before Sandro, partly disabled, could get to them, and before Colly could get out of his own bed.

The one sitting down was about 28. He looked as if he played a lot of tennis and went to bed early after parties. The other was a few years older. He looked more like a chess player.

Jenny's own gun was in a place where they would not have found it: but she was nowhere near the place and it might not help to have another gun being waved about in the room.

"Please forgive the intrusion, Miss Norrington," said the tennis player. "We have no wish to harm or alarm you."

"That's a relief," said Jenny. "P'raps in that case you'd be terribly sweet and point that gun somewhere else."

"No, I don't think I'll do that. Please tell us who you are and why you're here."

Jenny thought very quickly: if they know, why ask? The others haven't asked, in the bottling plant or by the lake or on the road. If they don't know then they're not that lot. They're a different lot. What are they after? Who are they?

Maybe they were not enemies at all. But the man on the bed still had a gun in his hand and it was still pointing at her.

There was laughter in the street below, the chords of a guitar and the wailing of some antique wind instrument.

Jenny opened her eyes to their widest extent. She let her mouth fall open too. She knew that this made her look half-witted: unable to give a rational answer to the simplest question. Usually it was a disguise but now it was a way of gaining time and putting them off their guard.

"Come along, Miss Norrington," said the chess player. His manner was impatient but not convincingly brutal.

Jenny gave signs of incipient hysteria. She opened and closed her mouth like a fish out of water. Her eyes goggled

154

and her shoulders shook. She took off one of her heavy wooden-soled sandals and inspected it with childish wonder.

The men looked nonplussed. But they were still there and still pointing guns at her.

A fly woke up and began to circle the bedroom. Jenny waved her sandal as though trying to swat it out of the air. She swatted the light bulb. It smashed. The room was in pitch darkness again. Jenny dropped to her hands and knees. She knew exactly where she was and where everything else was. She had her wooden sandal in her hand. She scampered like a spider round the edge of the room to where the bedside light was, the only other in the room. She smashed it with her shoe, then slid away from the bed into a corner. The men were thrashing about and swearing. One of them went to the windows. He pulled a curtain back. A little light came into the room. Not much, because the room faced back, away from the plaza, over an alley and some little houses and the Hotel Comercial, not enough to reveal Jenny as she crouched on the floor but enough to silhouette the man at the window. Jenny hit him on the side of the head very hard with her shoe. He went down. His gun rattled away over the tiled floor. Jenny ignored the gun. She dropped to the floor beside the bed in deep darkness. But the other man, as she expected, thought she would go for the gun. He went for it himself. As he bent to pick it up she rose to her knees and hit him on the side of the head. It was not such a good blow as the first. He grunted and staggered but he was not out. She hit him again and he was out.

Jenny opened the door of her bathroom and switched on the light in it. The tennis player was already regaining consciousness; the chess player would not be out long. Jenny put their guns in the pockets of her dressing gown, which was hanging up in the bathroom. She got her own gun from its hiding place, taped to the outside of the back of a bureau drawer which could not be pulled out of the bureau.

She unbolted the door and called down the passage to Sandro.

He would not come quickly but he would come.

She perched herself on the bureau, where she could see

155

both men. She put the gun down between her hairbrushes beside her. She lit a cigarette.

"Goddamnedest thing," said Colly. "Everything you said but completely different. Lovely equipment. I like that camera with an eye in the side of its head. I had a school teacher like that once, two pretty keen eyes in front and another at the—"

'Get on, stupid colonial," said Jenny.

"Yeah, well. These guys were hired by the outfit Cordle *bought*. How about that?"

"*How* about it?" asked Jenny.

"They were sent down here to peek at the new process we have. Elaborate cover, all pretty professional. Their firm was retained by Springtide. Springtide is an educational publisher. Cordle bought it earlier this year."

"Where we came in," said Jenny.

"That's right. So these boys not only did not spy on Dave Cordle, they turn out working for him. Well, for his ghost or his heirs or something."

"So they're clean."

"No, dirty, but only a little bit dirty, and not interested in us until they decided you had to be in the same line of business."

"That's part of what I don't understand."

"You carry something around, like the thing you have in your shirt, so your pals know where you are if you do something peculiar. Like for instance prowl around the police barracks at night."

"Is that what this thing was invented for?"

"It's not what it was invented for, but it's the only thing they could figure a civilian could possibly want to use it for."

"What do they think now?"

"They wonder how the hell it got there and *I* wonder how the hell it got there."

"Could they help, those two?"

"Not much. They tried. Sandro helped them try."

"Ugh."

"Not much of that either. They never heard of an industrial espionage outfit as large as the one we're interested in. They never heard of a fleet of cars all with trail-bugs beamed to each other, good idea as that undoubtedly is.

They never heard of guys with no identity at all, or of using these tiny electronic bugs the way they used one on you. They never heard of a salesman having a wreck in Troy, N.Y., or a machinery broker chasing his hat in the street in Pittsfield, Mass."

"You mean they say they didn't."

"They spoke the truth," said Sandro.

Jenny glanced at him. She did not want to know how Sandro was so sure. She said: "So the wrong mice walked into the mousetrap. What a bore. All that bashing about for nothing. It's done my shoe no good at all. I think they ought to replace it."

"They think you ought to replace their heads."

"It's a deal. I'll knit some in the morning. So meanwhile we send them packing?"

"They are packing now," said Sandro. "When they have finished packing they send themselves home to New York."

"Not California?"

"No," said Colly stiffly.

"I'm not saying anything," said Jenny. "Not a word. Are they sworn to secrecy?"

"Far from it."

"Oh I see. Yes, I see. Yes, all right. But they keep sending these execution squads, and it's all very frightening and messy, and we never know any more at the end."

"But this time, baby, we catch a few fish alive."

"How do we?"

"Because," said Sandro, "we have 3000 friends and *un alcalde* and a Chief of Police and a company of his police. Maybe we can certainly catch one alive."

"And then?"

"Whatever is necessary."

"Ugh."

"*Si, carissima,* but I want we should all live to be old, and we shall not without—"

"I know," said Jenny. "I still say 'ugh.' "

"In a check shirt, in a girl's check shirt," said Ty Matheson to a friend in a bar on Third Avenue. "And what a girl."

"Hot stuff?"

"A knockout," said Ty feelingly.

157

"In a check shirt," said the friend to his boss. "A girl's check shirt."

"One of our bugs?"

"Yes, no doubt about that. He described the signal."

"How did it get there, I wonder?"

"I put it there," said another executive present at the meeting.

"Ah. Then everything falls into place. Tucker gets Tucker Publishing to start this chimerical hare, this mythical indestructible paper, knowing someone will want to see how the trick is done . . . Tucker, Ganzarello and the girl all wait there. We'll accept the invitation. This time we want no mistake. This time I'll go myself."

Sandro's pursuit of the beautiful Ramona had become one of the town's jokes. The other girls of the town envied Ramona, more or less openly; some of the girls said that the huge Italian, though unfailingly *cortes*, was simply too ugly: but most found, as girls all over the world had found, that the sapphire-blue eyes in the big dark face were irresistibly fascinating: that he was altogether fascinating: that Ramona was as crazy as a lizard to keep on saying "no." Ramona was, for herself, much inclined to agree. But with a mother like Filomena she had no choice.

Sandro dressed up each evening, in his beautiful expensive clothes, for the comfortable ritual of the plaza. When the evenings were cool he wore a garment markedly less English than most of his clothes, a white coat, cut like a blazer, with large silver nautical buttons embossed with flags and anchors. The coat came from Milan, and looked it. White coats were the ultimate in chic in the plaza in the evening; it was the only white coat Sandro had with him. It was not really suitable. It smacked of the sea: or at least of those luxurious Mediterranean yacht-basins where yachts are for giving parties on rather than for sailing: but it looked very fine in the plaza, and attracted glances from all the girls. Ramona vastly admired the white coat. Even Filomena admired it. But her eyes did not soften nor her vigilance relax.

Slowly, slowly exercise was bringing back the muscles of Sandro's thigh. Jenny's left arm was pretty good but not yet strong. Colly still wearily dragged about his tons of plaster.

The arrival of the French party in the town was the most spectacular occurrence for years.

First came the telegrams, then a Spanish travel agent from Mexico City to inspect the accommodation of the Hotel Villanazul, and at last, in two immense cars, breathlessly awaited, M. and Mme. Desroches and their entourage.

Poor M. Desroches swelled the number of the town's invalids. He was in a wheel chair, the result of polio contracted in French West Africa where he had owned enormous estates. He was about 55, white haired, with the smooth pale face of a man who has been pampered all his life.

Mme. Desroches, by contrast, was wiry and active. She looked a few years older than her husband. Her coloring was almost Mexican, although she came from Western France, from La Rochelle.

There were, in addition, a valet-chauffeur, another chauffeur, a brow-beaten young male secretary, and a forbidding middle-aged maid. They were all French.

Other people who came to the town had a purpose in their visits. They were businessmen or sightseers, archaeologists or missionaries. The Desroches were magnificently purposeless. The *alcalde* obsequiously asked to what the town owed the honor of their visit; why, in a word, they had come to so small and obscure a place? The answer was: why not? There was no other answer. No other was needed.

Other visitors, even the most barbaric red-faced gringos, adapted themselves more or less to the routine of the town; it was a pleasant routine; to follow it made life easier. Not the Desroches. They brought their own routine with them. The hours they kept were the hours they were accustomed to keep, in Paris or Palm Beach, in Tokyo or Tampico. They were outrageously arrogant. They went noisily about the town, knocking at the shutters of shops which were closed, when the rest of the town was asleep; they went to sleep, demanding silence like Nero for his racehorse, when everybody else wanted to make a noise.

They made the Hotel Villanazul uncomfortable for the other residents and hell for the staff. They kept the place on the hop, in the middle of the night and in the hour of siesta. Their bells continuously rang. They descended to

bar and to kitchen with imperious demands in a language
no one could understand. Only the secretary spoke
Spanish, and he badly. He was not a man to be envied. The
valet, chauffeur and maid were not to be envied either but
the secretary had the worst of it because, by having to interpret, he brought down upon himself the odium of the
party's unreasonable demands.

They were not like any people the town had ever seen.
They stuck out like a sore thumb. Everybody watched them
and angrily discussed them. Stories of their outrages were
the principal topic in every bar, every evening, within
hours of their arrival. If they were aware of this they didn't
give a damn.

For a brief, heady period the Chief of Police thought M.
Desroches might be the cruel rich man from whom the
senorita ingles was fleeing. She assured him that it was not
so. Evidently he was not that man's minion either; he was
nobody's minion. He was a spoiled ill-tempered bully who
thought his money could buy everything. Unfortunately, in
so poor a town, he was right. In the eyes of God, perhaps,
his suffering and disability might excuse him; in the eyes of
the town nothing excused any member of the party.

The secretary told the *alcalde* that M. and Mme.
Desroches might stay for two weeks or three. The hearts of
the town sank. Money was not everything.

It was Sunday evening. The municipal band occupied
the cake-frill bandstand; their tubas and euphoniums filled
the plaza with the breezy noise of the band's small repertoire. The plaza was fullest on Sunday evenings. Farmers,
many of pure Indian blood, came into the town on Sunday
with or without their families. Extra tables were put out in
front of the cafes. The waiters flew to and fro with unusual
zest. The fizz and spit of frying tortillas was heard in each
cafe over the hubbub of conversation and laughter and
over the music of the municipal band; the smell of the
frying fat hung delightfully at the very level of the nose.
Hundreds of people sat at the tables of the cafes; hundreds
more strolled on the pink and blue tiles which paved the
sides of the plaza.

Even the Desroches, who had afflicted the town for five
days, were forgotten in the delights of Sunday evening.

Sandro, in his nautical white coat from Milan, limped

into the Cafe Tacambaro from his table outside the cafe. He chatted to Ramona. Ramona was very hot and busy frying tortillas, but she smiled. Dozens of people saw the exchange. Dozens of people saw Ramona smile and then, under her mother's watchful eye, firmly shake her head.

Afterwards the people said that they saw, on Sandro's face as he limped back to the table, an expression of ferocity and of despair.

"What exactly are your intentions, fatty?" asked Jenny when he sat down. She leaned her head close to his ear to speak, without shouting, against the oompahs of the band. She glanced at Ramona as she spoke.

"All the time I learn," said Sandro. "I learn Spanish, I learn how to make tortillas, I learn what it is like to be *mestizo* and to live in a town like this town."

He also glanced at Ramona and Filomena, frowning to think what they had managed to survive. Two of Ramona's brothers had died of tuberculosis; her sister had died within minutes of her birth; her father had been run over and killed by a German tourist who was drunk.

Dozens of people saw the conversation between Jenny and Sandro. They were not prying. Watching other people was part of the entertainment of a Sunday evening in the plaza. Afterwards they reported that Jenny whispered to Sandro while glancing at Ramona; that Sandro whispered back, glancing also at Ramona, frowning, they all afterwards agreed, like a *demente*, a *maniatico*.

It was a long night. The town kept late hours on Sunday. The band at last put away its instruments and some of the cafes put up their shutters, but there was laughter and singing in the plaza almost until dawn.

Ramona's body was found at five in the morning.

161

CHAPTER FOURTEEN

The policeman Esteban was off duty but in his uniform. He was in his uniform because he had gone to sleep in a corner of the plaza instead of in his bed at home. He was woken by a kick: not, probably, deliberate: merely the ill-directed stumble of a late-drinking citizen of the town who was doing his best to go to his bed now that the sky was becoming pale in the east.

Esteban yawned, rubbed his eyes, and stretched. He thought of his bed and the anger of his wife that he had not returned to it. His mouth felt like the inside of the den of an evil-smelling animal; his tongue felt as furry as the animal itself. His head ached. He was very stiff from sleeping on the hard stones of the plaza. He should have left his friends earlier; he should have gone home to bed; he wished very hard that he had done so.

The choice now faced Esteban of going home or going to the station. Each plan had advantages and drawbacks. He got unsteadily to his feet, undecided. His headache was worse when he stood up.

Still undecided, he stumbled up an alley off the plaza which was the first stage of the journey to either home or station. Another alley branched off to the left. He found himself going along it, back to his fat wife Maria, although voices in his head warned him that this was not the best or safest plan.

The alley ran past the back of the Cafe Tacambaro. Luis

and Filomena and the others had stacked a lot of rubbish behind the cafe. Some of the rubbish would doubtless stay there for ever, becoming part of the permanent structure of the town. Some would have to be removed. There were ordinances in the matter, often restated if seldom obeyed.

Amongst the rubbish, protruding from below a loose stack of empty cardboard boxes, was a small brown bare foot.

Esteban stopped and blinked. No explanation came at once to his fuddled mind.

He jogged the foot with the toe of his own boot. It wagged limply. The owner of the foot was more deeply asleep than Esteban had been.

A thought entered Esteban's head which filled him with fascinated horror. He began pitching the cartons away, anywhere, all over the place, in his anxiety to see what lay below them.

Ramona lay in the middle of the litter of cartons and of the other rubbish which had been pushed out of the back of the Cafe Tacambaro. She was dead. There had been a struggle. She had fought. Nearly all her clothes had been pulled off; only a fragment of her blouse whisped round her shoulders. There was a narrow leather belt tight round her neck, a distinctive belt of plaited yellow hide. She had been strangled with the belt. There was some blood, although it seemed she had been killed by strangling rather than by stabbing or blows. One of her legs was straight; one knee was drawn up. There was blood between them. She had been raped with great ferocity before her death. Her arms were behind her, pulled back under her body. Esteban thought her wrists were tied together, but he did not think it proper to move the body in order to see.

Esteban sobbed with horror and with sadness for Ramona. He felt a great anger and he wanted to vomit.

It was still cool. The sky was not yet fully bright. Neither heat nor flies would attack the poor body for a while.

Esteban covered up the body with sheets of newspaper which were flapping about the alley behind the cafe. Then he ran to the police station.

The station was deserted. There were no prisoners in the cells. No one had been arrested in the night. Although many men had been drunk no crime, except the rape and

163

murder of Ramona, had been committed. Two men at least should have been on duty but they were not at their posts.

Esteban forced himself to think. He ran to the house of the Chief of Police, a nice house with fresh whitewash. The house was entirely dark and quiet. Esteban banged on the door. He woke the whole of the street before he got any response from the house of the Chief of Police. Heads came out of windows, the sleep-softened tousled heads of people woken rudely from their dreams. The people were angry and cursed Esteban. But he knew his duty and he banged on the door and shouted.

At last the shutter swung open above the door. Its hinges squeaked and it slammed against the white wall. The wife of the Chief of Police poked her head furiously out of the window. She began to rail at the noise-maker until she saw that it was Esteban. She still railed at him but in a different way as he was a member of the police. He got it through to her that he must talk, and at once, to the Chief.

The exchange, shouted from street to window, brought still more heads out of the windows of the street. A few men, half-dressed, pulling on their thin cotton trousers, came out into the street to see and hear more closely what was going on. The street was filling with pearly light from the sky.

After another long interval the Chief of Police thrust his head out of the upstairs window and cursed Esteban. He looked very sleepy. His eyes were gummed with sleep and he had great difficulty in speaking and in thinking. He refused to come downstairs to the door so that Esteban could address him confidentially. He accused Esteban of being drunk. He demanded an explanation of his subordinate's outrageous conduct.

Esteban shouted that there had been a murder. This brought the Chief of Police down to the door of his house. It brought most of the rest of the street down to the doors of their houses also. The street became full of people, sleepy but excited, not yet horrified because they did not yet know what Esteban knew.

Esteban and the Chief of Police tried to have a private conversation in the doorway but it was impossible. The people pressed round them and heard most of what was said. They heard that Ramona Licon had been savagely murdered and that her body lay in the alley behind the

164

Cafe Tacambaro. The crowd began to pour towards the place. The crowd was like a tidal wave in a narrow and rocky river. The men were muttering with anger. Ramona had been known as the most beautiful girl in the town, and as a girl of the most perfect virtue owing to her mother Filomena.

"The body must not be touched!" screamed the Chief of Police.

He ordered Esteban to get to the place before the crowd destroyed all the evidence. He ordered another man to run for the doctor. He ordered one of his daughters to get his trousers.

Esteban tried to push through the roaring crowd. He shouted as he ran that the body must not be touched. Clues must be left undisturbed, he shouted, or the murderer would not be caught. Esteban was allowed to reach the back of the Cafe Tacambaro before the crowd. The men understood about clues and about catching the murderer. Their cold anger against the murderer made them wish very hard for him to be identified. Esteban stood guard over the body until the Chief of Police and the doctor came to examine it. The crowd filled the narrow alley on both sides of the cafe's untidy back, leaving a little space for Esteban and the body.

It was almost full day.

The great bell of the Cathedral thundered once; a cloud of pigeons exploded out of the bell tower like spray from a wave; the pigeons flew at high speed round the plaza, caught by the first rays of the rising sun, and settled again on the roof of the Cathedral.

The Chief of Police and the doctor pushed with difficulty through the crowd to the back of the cafe. The Chief of Police was now wide awake and decently dressed. The doctor was still three-quarters asleep. They advanced to the place where Esteban was standing guard over a pile of newspapers. The doctor said that if there was a body under the newspapers, which he did not at all believe, it would have to be moved very soon because of the heat and flies.

Esteban removed the sheets of rustling newspaper. He uncovered the body. The crowd pressed forward, awed, murmuring. There was a growl of rage from the crowd. The Chief of Police looked sick but he ordered the crowd back so that he and the doctor could examine the corpse.

The crowd was much swollen. Word had flown to other streets.

The doctor said Ramona had been dead only a short time. Rigor mortis had set in. She had in any case been working at the Cafe Tacambaro until two o'clock or maybe later. She had been killed in the small hours of the morning, maybe at four. There was still so much noise in that part of the town at four o'clock that her screams, if she screamed, would not have been noticed.

The motive of the murder was obvious. There was no room for doubt.

Ramona's wrists were tied together behind her back with a piece of silk. It was a scarf, pale-blue with a pattern of red poppies. It was foreign and strange. It was not an object likely to belong to anybody who lived in the town. Nobody had seen it before.

The belt which had strangled Ramona was also unknown to the police, the doctor, or the crowd. No one had ever seen before a belt made of plaited strips of yellow leather. It was totally unfamiliar, a foreign thing like the scarf, something brought by a visitor.

Who? Why and how were obvious. When was sufficiently obvious. But who?

The discussion should have been limited to the Chief of Police, the doctor, and Esteban, but all the men in the forefront of the crowd joined in. They were concerned. It was their affair. They had known Ramona in life and they would avenge her in death.

A man counted on his fingers. He said: "There are 12 foreigners in the town."

"So many?"

"Think. The three Americans of the printing in the old barracks. The American with broken limbs, the Italian, the English girl. That is six. And the French, six of them, to make 12."

The angry murmur of the crowd began to rise in pitch like a lethal machine being accelerated.

"Silence! Order!" shouted the Chief of Police. "You are going too fast. This must be left to the police."

"The foreigners. The 12 foreigners."

"Perhaps. And perhaps not, *idiotas*. How do we know that the belt and the piece of silk were not stolen from one of the foreigners?"

166

"It is possible . . ."

"We will ask them which of them owns these things."

"All of us will ask."

"Certainly. All of us will go at once to the foreigners and demand the truth—"

"The foreigners will be asked this and many other questions," shouted the Chief of Police, "and by me, in proper form, at the correct time."

A man said: "I was, last night, at the Cafe Tacambaro."

"And I."

"I also."

"I saw, speaking to Ramona, *el italiano grande*."

"*El grueso*. I saw."

"And I."

"For weeks he has been trying to debauch her."

"Every day, for weeks."

"I have seen that."

"We have all seen it. Everybody knows it."

"He looks a man of great impatience and hotness."

"A man of great strength, a bull."

"Last night he tried again with Ramona."

"We saw him try at the cafe."

"She said no."

"As always."

"She shook her head thus, to say no."

"I confirm that she did."

"I too."

"He returned to his friends."

"To the gringo and the English girl."

"He was angry."

"His face was dark with anger."

"He was impatient. He would wait no longer."

"He sat down and they whispered together."

"He and the English girl."

"That is true. I saw it."

"They cast glances at Ramona."

"Both did so as they whispered. I saw it clearly."

"I saw everything that you describe. It was exactly as you say."

"He frowned."

"It was the frown of a madman."

"Greedy, furious."

"He is an ape, a monster."

"Lustful. Insensate."

"Drunk. Beside himself."

"The others helped him."

"It is her silken scarf. It must be."

"I have seen her wearing it about her head."

"Are you certain?" asked the Chief of Police.

"It seems to me that I saw it on her head."

"I have the same impression."

"No one else has been seen to wear it. That is quite certain."

"I too am positive of that."

"The belt?"

"I picture it round the waist of the American."

"It is easy to picture."

"I do not picture it round any other waist."

"It has encircled no other waist."

"We can all swear to that."

A stretcher was now brought, not before time, to take the poor remains to the police station. There the doctor would make a fuller and further examination. Then, as soon as possible, Ramona would be buried.

The body was still completely flaccid. It was lifted, respectfully, by many hands, on to the stretcher. A hush had fallen over the crowd.

As she was lifted, Ramona's hands fell limply away from her body. One of them unclenched. Something fell on to the cobbles of the alley, something which gleamed in the pale morning sun.

It was a large silver button, embossed with an anchor and a flag.

A simultaneous howl rose from those who could see. It was taken up by the rest, pressing forward but too far away to see. It was the howl of the pack, of the lynch-mob.

"Be still! Wait!" screamed the Chief of Police. "A great error might be made! Another murder must not be committed, of a man who may be innocent, and by you! I order you to wait! I beg you to wait!"

The howl diminished in volume but the crowd was in an angry and vengeful mood. Some of the men hurried away to their homes to get machetes and rifles. A man went for a piece of rope.

Soledad, oldest and most respected of the chambermaids at the Hotel Villanazul, was hobbling to work past the cor-

ner of the alley when the men went away to get their
weapons. She asked a man what was going on, who was at-
tacking the town, from what quarter the enemy was coming.

He said that the gross Italian madman and his friends
were about to be executed for a disgusting murder.

Soledad gasped, and ran as she had not run for years to
the Hotel Villanazul.

Usually Jenny woke up very quickly and was fully
awake in a second. But her night had been short. Although
her room faced to the back, away from the plaza, a lot of
noise had come into the room until a very late hour. She
did not mind the noise. She was glad the people of the
town had such a good time on Sunday night. But it prevented her from sleeping until almost dawn. When Soledad
burst into her room she was slower than usual in waking,
slower to grasp the agonized urgency of what Soledad was
saying.

As soon as she understood she flew to Colly's room and
Sandro's.

The Chief of Police had sent for more of his men, for his
whole force of eight men. Between them they managed to
restrain the crowd. The Chief of Police was hoarse with
shouting, with beseeching and commanding the men of the
town not to commit another murder.

Four men from the crowd, with a very numerous reti-
nue, began to carry the body of Ramona on the stretcher
to the police station. A deep silence fell.

Shutters opened in a crumbling adobe wall opposite the
back of the Cafe Tacambaro. An aged head appeared. It
was Jorge, once a strong young man, now an ill-tempered
eccentric who spoke to no one. He never left his house; he
took no interest in the outside world. He was very angry
that his sleep had been disturbed.

He made one of his rare speeches. He said: "A noise like
the devils of hell at four in the morning and a greater noise
at seven in the morning. It is not to be borne. You are all
pigs."

"What noise at four? What did you hear?"

"The screams of a she-devil. The grunting of a man, a
noise like a great pig."

The men in the crowd all looked at one another. Jorge had heard everything. Had he seen?

He had seen a fight. It was nothing remarkable among the pigs of the town on a Sunday night. Pigs and she-devils had fought in the street. The police should have prevented it, but doubtless they were all drunk.

"Who fought, Jorge?"

"How do I know? It was dark. I know nobody. I see nobody. Nobody ever comes to see me, thanks be to God."

"What did they look like, those who fought?"

"It was dark, fool. Two men and two women. A dark woman screamed. Doubtless a slut, like all women in this town. She was, I think the she-devil who constantly disturbs my peace by banging the door at the back of that stinking and dishonest cafe."

"Ramona."

"How do I know? And there was a *rubia. Una puta rubia.*"

"How do you know?"

"All women in this pig's town are prostitutes. I did not see the face of this one. There was a dark man in a white coat. I did not see his face. And a man with a leg as though of white stone—"

"Plaster."

"How do I know?"

The police were swept aside.

The crowd did not run. No man hurried. The time for suspicion was past, for hysteria, for shouting and howling to cover doubt. There was no more doubt to cover. The Chief of Police had brayed incessantly that they must be certain, that there must be evidence. Now there was evidence and they were quite certain. Every man knew what had to be done.

A great variety of weapons was carried by the crowd. There were 40 or 50 rifles, very many machetes, knives, meat-cleavers, spikes and clubs. There were several long pieces of rope.

The crowd assembled, many hundreds strong, in the plaza. It advanced at a seemly pace, and in seemly silence towards the Hotel Villanazul.

CHAPTER FIFTEEN

Jenny and Sandro pulled a few clothes on to themselves and on to Colly.

From Colly's window Jenny saw the silent, orderly crowd crossing the plaza from the Cathedral to the Hotel Villanazul. She saw the rifles. The sun filled half the plaza with its brilliant dry white light; the light reflected on the blades of machetes and cleavers and knives.

Three men, two with rifles, broke away from the crowd and walked without haste up the side alley from which the back of the Hotel Villanazul could be reached. Soon the three would be outside the back entrances and below Jenny's balcony.

"We must get there before," said Sandro gently.

"Yes. I'll go."

"I will go."

"Can you darling?"

"We will see."

Part of the archeological equipment, for use in exploring caves and cliff faces, was a length of slim nylon rope. Jenny knotted one end to a leg of her bed. Sandro pushed the bed to the door on to Jenny's balcony so that it was jammed across the door. He pushed the coil of rope between the bars of the balcony railing; it unwound as it flopped down the side of the hotel.

There was no sound in the hotel. All the servants had fled or hidden. They did not wish to join the crowd in the execution; they did not at all wish to oppose the crowd. There was no sound from the French party on the floor below; it was too early for them to be stirring. If the other guests of the hotel knew what was happening they pulled their bedclothes over their heads.

Sandro went down the nylon rope using his hands only. He could not grip with his wounded leg. He descended softly, like a giant leopard, on to one of the low roofs of the outhouses of the hotel, which formed a little jumbled village below the walls of the hotel like a hamlet below the walls of a medieval castle.

Jenny watched Sandro down. As soon as she saw that he was safely on his little roof (and she prayed that it was strong enough to bear his great weight) Jenny pulled the rope up again. She tied a loop in the middle of the rope and placed the loop around Colly's chest. She threaded the free end of the rope round another leg of the bed. She did not drop the rope to Sandro again because it would give them away to the men who were coming to guard the back of the hotel.

The men turned the corner into the alley which led to the jumbled outbuildings behind the hotel. The three had become five. There were three rifles, a gleaming sickle, and a long heavy tool like a kind of mattock.

Sandro sheltered behind a low adobe wall, tile-topped, which extended two and a half feet above the flat roof of his outbuilding. It was pierced so that water could run off the roof into the alley. Sandro could see through one of the narrow drains in the wall. If necessary he could shoot through it but he did not want to shoot because the noise would bring a hundred men. He was himself in deep shadow. He was sure he could not be seen through the drain. The alley ran north and south; it lay to the west of the tall bulk of the hotel; it was in deep blue-brown shadow cast by the early sun.

The five men stationed themselves by the various back doors of the hotel, the main back door and the doors into the fuel store, meal store, larders and other sheds and lean-tos. The men looked conscientious. They were as determined as all the rest of the crowd to avenge Ramona. They guarded the back of the hotel effectively with their rifles and other weapons. They did not expect a party to descend from a high window which included a man who

172

limped, a man with an arm and a leg in plaster, and a girl.

Sandro knew that by now the crowd would have reached the front door of the hotel. The men in the forefront of the crowd would be entering, quietly and with dignity, with no wish to upset the other residents but only to find and execute the guilty.

Below Sandro a man moved round the corner of the little building. He was stationed where he could see the open door of a shack stacked high with empty bottles and the closed door of a privy. He could not see his friends. It was a sensible position to take up if the people he was hunting could not climb out of high windows.

Sandro moved softly on to the sloping tiles of the next little roof. He peeped over the edge of the roof and the man was directly below him. All Sandro could see was a broad brimmed straw hat, tattered all round the edge of the brim, and the barrel of an old-fashioned army rifle. The crown of the hat was five feet below Sandro.

The hat had to be got out of the way, but at the right moment and not an instant before.

Sandro took from his pocket the spool of fine nylon fishing line. It had very many uses, of which Sandro's present use was a new one. He tied the end of the line to the narrow loop on the handle of his cosh. He cut off ten feet of the line. He cut off another ten feet and to the end of his new piece tied a .38 shell.

He made these preparations extremely quickly.

The men in the van of the lynch mob would not blunder all over the hotel, killing or terrorizing indiscriminately, like the Egyptian mob in Shepheard's Hotel in Cairo. They would try to find the correct rooms with the minimum of fuss. But there would be no staff for them to ask, and they would not understand the hotel register even if it were lying about in the foyer. Confident that the back of the hotel was guarded, they would proceed with as much tact as possible to locating their quarry.

Sandro had a little time: but only a very little.

In his left hand he lowered the bullet on its nylon line until it nudged the tattered straw brim of the hat below. He bounced the bullet gently on the straw of the hat; he made it behave like a sleepy beetle, a puzzled but torpid insect.

The man might have reacted in many ways, but he reacted in the way that suited Sandro best. He took off his hat. Immediately Sandro swung the cosh, at the end of the other piece of fishing line, as an English schoolboy swings a horse chestnut conker at another which dangles on its string. He hit the man on the side of the skull. The man went down.

Sandro did not want to hurt these men, who were decent and honorable. But he would do what was necessary as long as they wanted to kill him.

The man collapsed quietly, a limp pile of loose white cotton, stringly teak-brown arms, thin *mestizo* face with ferocious moustache. The rifle clattered on to the cobbles of the alley.

"Jose?" called a voice.

Another of the men hurried round a corner. He saw Jose unconscious on the ground. He looked wildly round. He looked up. Sandro was out of sight. He peeped cautiously into the door behind which all the bottles were stacked. He rattled the closed door of the privy. He wore a small, very battered panama hat. Sandro ignored the hat. He swung his cosh at the head he could not quite see below the hat. The second man went down beside the first. His rifle made no clatter because it fell on Jose.

Sandro glanced up at Jenny's balcony. Neither she nor Colly was to be seen. They had to hide from the sight of the other men guarding the back of the hotel.

There was very little time. The sun was climbing. Every minute would wake other streets, and bring men with rifles and machetes from all directions towards the hotel.

Sandro crawled from roof to roof of the little huddled outbuildings. He moved as quietly as always but slowly because of his wounded leg.

He hoped he would see another man alone but he saw below him two men together. They were solemn and alert, not talking, watching and listening.

With the .38 shell on the end of its piece of nylon line Sandro imitated a beetle dancing clumsily on the big straw hat of one of the men. The man took off his hat. Sandro swung the cosh at his head at the end of five feet of fishing line and knocked him out. His mattock rattled on to the cobbles beside him.

The other man looked upwards immediately, raising his rifle.

Sandro gritted his teeth and jumped on the man. He

174

landed directly on top of the man, knocking his rifle away and bearing him to the ground. Sandro knocked the man out with the heel of his hand. He drew his own gun.

Where was the fifth?

The fifth called out and came running.

Sandro was ready for him. As he rounded the corner of the fuel house Sandro tackled him low. He crashed to the ground. His sickle skittered noisily away over the cobbles. Sandro hurt his own bad leg. The man's head hit the cobbles.

Sandro stood up painfully and signaled to the dark oblong of Jenny's window.

Jenny had run to Sandro's room and to Colly's and locked them from the outside. From Colly's window, peeping cautiously out into the low sun and with her unmistakable head shrouded in a dark shirt, she had seen the crowd densely packed at the front of the hotel. From the landing she had heard the voices of the crowd in the hall below, murmuring, talking reasonably, not shouting; they lost none of their dignity in anger; they embarked on a lynching soberly and with decorum.

Jenny listened out of the open door of her room while Colly covertly watched out of her window. Jenny heard the voices of the first two dozen men of the crowd as they came up the first flight of stairs. She stopped listening. She locked her own door and moved a chest against it. She could not move the bed because it was needed where it was. The wardrobe was too heavy for her to move and Colly was unable to help with one good leg and arm.

Jenny wondered very much what Sandro was doing. But she could not go out on the balcony to see.

The sound of a shot would mean failure. Another sound might mean failure or success. Silence was probably success. There was no sound from below: a minor rattle, a name softly called, no panic or stampede, no cry of triumph.

She edged forward so that she could see down into the alley without being seen. Something white lay on the ground. It looked like a leg in Mexican cotton pants.

Time passed which seemed a very long time. There were knocks on doors on the floor below; then a few voices. An indignant scream seemed to be in the voice of the sour French maid of Mme. Desroches.

Voices came nearer. They were coming up the stairs to the floor where Jenny and Colly were, the first squad of the army below, the squad which would arrest for the army to execute, men coldly angry and utterly certain, men with secret, graven brown faces, with the ancient dignity of their Indian ancestors and the moral rigidity of their Spanish inheritance, men who would in a short time catch them and kill them, a great army of men, a large part of the population of the town.

Of all imaginable enemies these dignified, impoverished townspeople were the most implacable.

Jenny saw Sandro limp out from the cover of the shanties below. He walked stiffly, painfully. He looked up and grinned.

"All clear aft," said Colly.

There were knocks on the doors further down the corridor.

Sandro saw Jenny come out on to the balcony. She tossed the coiled nylon rope far out so that it landed clear of the outbuildings. Sandro picked up the rope. Jenny and Colly between them somehow got Colly over the balustrade of the balcony. Sandro took the strain and lowered Colly as quickly as he dared. Colly, helpless, the rope under his arms, revolved slowly as he went down the side of the hotel. Sandro tried to deposit him gently on the roof where he had himself landed.

Jenny, from above, saw Colly subside on to the roof. The knocking on the doors of the corridors was nearer. She undid the knot which attached the nylon rope to the bed leg, but left the rope looped behind the other leg. She went like a cat over the balustrade of the balcony, and like a monkey down the doubled rope. As she went down she heard the knocking at her own door.

Colly got himself to the edge of the little roof. He hauled himself on to the low wall which surrounded it. Sandro stretched up his arms. Colly let himself fall four feet into Sandro's arms. Sandro could not keep his balance when he caught Colly because of the weakened muscles of his leg. He subsided backwards on to the ground under Colly's weight. He prevented Colly from hurting himself.

"Nice fly catch, boy," said Colly. "Right in the mitt."

Jenny was already on the little roof. She pulled the rope

176

down and tossed it to Sandro. She slipped over the low wall and joined them in the alley.

There was a crash from above as the crowd knocked over the furniture she had pulled in front of her door. In a moment there would be faces on her balcony.

"Hats, rifles, ponchos," said Sandro.

By keeping close under the walls of the outbuildings they could stay out of sight from the few windows of the hotel which gave onto the back. From the five unconscious men they took the three biggest straw sombreros. Only one had a poncho. Jenny pulled it on. She pulled her hair into the crown of her big hat. She was spectacularly fair by contrast with the people of the town even with her hair hidden. She rubbed dirt on to her face and the backs of her hands. Sandro was far bigger than any of the men of the town. But at least his face was deeply tanned after weeks of the Mexican sun. Colly's plaster, on arm and leg, was concealed. They were disguised well enough for a fleeting glance from a distance, but not better than that.

Jenny and Sandro took rifles from the men on the cobblestones. Colly took the mattock because it might help him to get along.

What they wanted was a car, their own or any other. When cars came to the town they were parked in a space behind the Opera House. The town had few cars of its own.

They started for the cobbled parking area, where there was a one-man service station and a gas pump. It was a long way round, avoiding the plaza and the alleys nearest the plaza. If they got away in a car they would be arrested eventually but it was better to be arrested by the police than lynched by the crowd.

They knew the town well. They were able to use alleys and archways, narrow footpaths like drains between houses, and the deep shadows in the gaps between buildings. Most of the town was by now in the plaza. A lot of the buildings were already empty. The little stores in the alleys were not yet open; they would not open at all today because the town had other business. Children and old women were left in the houses of the people. Looking down from the windows of the houses they saw only the wide tattered brims of the sombreros, and the weapons which all men were carrying today.

They had to knock out, in an alley, one man who recognized them; and hurry away from the piping cries of an old woman who saw Colly's limp; otherwise they were lucky.

Their luck ran out. A dozen men with rifles and other weapons guarded the cars in the open space behind the Opera House.

"We walk," said Sandro, without apparent dismay.

Colly began to get very tired and Sandro's leg hurt but they made it to the edge of the town, to the deserted shacks of the poorest Indians who camped there, who now stood, dignified and silent and angry, with the enormous crowd in the plaza.

A hundred yards away, up a steep path lined with tall cactus, gleamed the fat white adobe wall of the cemetery, with stone angels at each end and a wrought iron gate in the middle.

Sandro and Jenny glanced from the cemetery to Colly.

"Let's hit the trail," said Colly with difficulty.

The path was stony and covered with fine white dust. It was too narrow for them to go three abreast. Sandro and Jenny could not support Colly from each side. Sandro grabbed the belt at the back of Colly's pants and half lifted him along the steep track. Sandro's own leg hurt badly.

Jenny had overused her wounded arm in helping Colly over the rail of her balcony and in coming down the rope herself. It was not much use to her.

They labored up the track. The sun rose higher, shortening the long blue shadows of the cactus. Colly's face was white with pain and fatigue. Jenny was pouring with sweat; it streaked the dirt she had rubbed on her face. The spines of the cactus plucked at their sleeves and skin.

Bodies were not carried to the cemetery by this route. There was a much longer way, a broad and gently sloping path suitable for processions and pallbearers. This was the shortcut used by widows who came to put flowers on a grave, and by children paying the annual rent to the caretaker for their parents' graves.

It was already very hot, a parching white heat as dry as the white dust which coated their shoes and clung to their faces. The breath rasped in their throats, dry dusty air as hot as the metal of the rifles. Sandro was limping heavily; his sleeve was shredded by the cactus spines.

178

They had only a short way to go, 20 yards threaded between the tall, contorted cactus, 20 shingly uneven yards up a steep incline to the iron gate in the cemetery wall.

There was the sound of a shot from 80 yards behind. A bullet slapped into the adobe wall.

"I think they maybe want us alive," said Sandro. *"Andiam, caro."*

He struggled up the last few yards, lifting Colly almost clear of the ground.

Jenny turned. A small group of men stood by the sudden squalid edge of the town, where it turned, in the course of a yard, into desert. A rifle was raised. There was a puff of smoke. The flash was invisible in the brilliant sunlight. Jenny heard the report and the slam of the bullet into the ground a few feet to her right. Sandro had guessed correctly. They were shooting to capture, to cow, maybe to wound, but not to kill. Death by bullet was too honorable for what Sandro and his friends were believed to have done.

Jenny raised the old rifle. But she did not want to shoot. There was no point in killing or hurting one man or 50 in a force of a thousand. There was no possibility of frightening the whole army away.

Jenny lowered her rifle and scrambled up the last few yards of track after the others. They went through the gate into the graveyard.

"They have debauched our living. Now they desecrate our dead."

"It is a fortress."

"It is also a trap."

"A trap without food or water."

"Yes, we shall use the ropes."

"Does everybody understand that they are not to shoot?"

"We will make certain that everybody understands."

The message was passed from man to man, not an order but a general decision; every man nodded as he heard the message, all the men of the town who now stood, in an enormous single rank, at the edge of the town, at the foot of the hillside on which the cemetery stood. Every man agreed that, if a rifle had to be used, it was not to be used to kill.

The *alcalde* and the Chief of Police blustered up and down the long, long line of silent men. They shouted about the law, evidence, procedures, judges, penalties. The men of the town listened with polite indifference. The *alcalde* and the Chief of Police were eminent and respected, men of education: but while they were learned they had, it appeared, forgotten.

There was no leader. There was no need for a leader. The men were united in anger and in purpose. No one could afterwards say that he, Ureta, or he, Ysotl, was ringleader, and had incited his fellows to this illegal act. The town needed no inciting. It had a community of will like a swarm of insects or a flock of plovers.

A man said, in a tone of mild surprise: *"He aqui el frances grosero."*

The uncouth Frenchman had indeed come in his wheel-chair to the edge of the town. He was pushed by his valet and flanked by his secretary. Fifty faces turned to look at him stolidly. He was neither welcome nor unwelcome, but irrelevant.

Through his secretary, M. Desroches explained to those nearest that he had heard, from the men who searched the hotel, of the outrage committed in the small hours of the morning. He was deeply shocked. He was ashamed that a visitor from his own continent of Europe should so have abused the hospitality of the town.

Two dozen men listened to the secretary in silence. They turned back, without reply or any change of expression, to face the cemetery. They were neither gratified nor irritated by the Frenchman's speech. They were not interested in anything he thought. This was not his affair but theirs.

The men began to move, although no order was given. Each flank began to extend itself round the cemetery. The men moved slowly. They picked their way, in their sandals, over rough ground and cactus. There was no hurry. Nobody could climb over the four-square adobe walls without being seen, or run away across the arid hillside. One of those among the tombs could not run; one could only walk with difficulty. The town could take its time.

M. Desroches said something in his harsh, peremptory voice, to his valet. The valet began to wheel him towards the cemetery, by the longer route which funerals took, which the municipal band took on the occasion of the

180

fiesta of *el dia de Muerte,* the broad path which was smooth enough for wheels. The wheelchair was in the midst of the left flank of the army of the town. The soldiers of the army ignored it.

Presently, when the sun was high, the cemetery was surrounded. No voice was raised. No voice had been raised, of command, anger, grief, derision or defiance. A thousand carved teak Spanish Indian faces gazed, from all points, at the cemetery, at the four slab walls, the large and the small iron gates, and the wind-eroded angels on the four corners.

When the ring was complete it began to draw inwards. A thousand men began, very slowly to walk across the hillside towards the cemetery.

CHAPTER SIXTEEN

In many poor places the promise of eternal bliss is all that makes life bearable. Life is the never-ending struggle against dry and stony ground, or the never-ending lash of the slave master's bullhide whip. Life has to be sustained by hope, and the only hope is death. The negro slaves sang of crossing Jordan into the Promised Land. In the south of Italy the dead lie in marble houses more luxurious and ornate by far than anything they see in life. But life is short and eternity long; there is commonsense in this scale of values.

In this hillside cemetery of a small poor Mexican town many of the graves were astonishingly rich and ornate. Marble angels, florid headstones many feet high, great slabs like ornate flowerbeds, crosses and ironwork remembered those who lay below ground. There were also marble sarcophagi above ground, massive, baroque in decoration, many raised high above the gravel on stone sleepers. Still others of the dead lay in slots in the thick walls of the cemetery, sealed into the walls with memorial plaques, families together.

Everywhere, on headstones, coffins and slabs, were tacked or hung the small possessions of the dead, their treasures, little brass crucifixes, holy pictures, bracelets and bangles given for first communions, passports to Paradise, things they might require, like the boats and spears and hunting chariots of Tutenkhamun.

The graveyard was tidy, gravel well-raked, marble,

smooth white dust, tiled walks in fondant colors like the footpaths which edged the plaza of the town. The sun beat down on the happy dead and the unhappy living. It glared pitilessly off the polished marble and the matt white of the adobe, off brass and fine white dust.

Jenny peeped through the larger wrought iron gate which gave to the broad ceremonial track from the town to the cemetery, and through the small one which gave to the steep track through the cactus. She saw that the men of the town stood like a palisade round the cemetery: erect, immobile, white and brown, in a complete circle. The sun blinked on rifle barrels and edged steel weapons.

"That's it, then," said Jenny.

"I'm afraid it is, baby," said Colly.

"Soledad didn't make much sense. What actually had happened?"

"Somebody killed little Ramona when she came off duty at the cafe. They stole one of Sandro's buttons and put it in the poor kid's hand."

"And somebody says they saw us?"

"Yeah. In the dark somebody saw a big guy in a white coat. A dame with a lot of blonde hair. And a leg in a lot of white bandages. Add that to the button. Add that to Sandro pretending to proposition Ramona most evenings. Add all of that to us being foreigners."

"You can't really blame the people."

"I try not to. But I'm not in that league for charity."

"Who did it?"

"We will never know," said Sandro. "It is most extremely annoying."

"The goddam irony is," said Colly, "our mousetrap worked, second time around, and now it's about to kill us."

"Yes," said Jenny. "And I thought we'd thought of everything."

"Pretty near everything. But not poor little Ramona being killed in an alley by a bunch looking like us. We didn't think dirty enough. Ah well. You get the breaks, you don't get the breaks. We had a pretty good run these last few years."

"Pretty good," said Jenny.

"What does annoy me a little is, whoever did it ends up with completely clean hands."

Sandro nodded. "When we are dead the case of Ramona
183

is closed. And while we are becoming dead, our man is a bystander, innocent, not part of the lynching. Or at the most one of a crowd of one thousand men."

"Good gracious," said Jenny, peeping again through the larger gate. She was very frightened, but she struggled to show, in face and voice, the calmness that Sandro and Colly showed. As evenly and chattily as she could she said: "There is a bystander. A bysitter. That rude frog."

"Then he's it," said Colly instantly.

"Credo di si," said Sandro. "He comes to see his very clever plan complete."

"Oh no," said Jenny. "He's just morbid, like the crowds at Tyburn. He couldn't be our man. I mean, if you come to a place, a small place like this, to kill some people, you don't carry on like that. It's crazy. He arrives in a great party in vast cars, and never for a second stops drawing attention to himself, and gets himself loathed by everybody—surely a man who . . . oh."

"Exactly," said Colly. "Double bluff. The people you suspect are people like us, who fit in with the place, or like the phoney geologists, who bring a waterproof cover and a good reason to be here."

"But I don't know any Frenchmen with polio," said Jenny. "Do you know any Frenchmen with polio?"

"I guess," said Colly, "we can assume he's no Frenchman and he never had any polio."

"He sounds French to me," said Jenny.

"Anche me."

"I mean, if he's not French, he's a bloody good linguist."

"Yeah?" said Colly. "I take your word for it. My ear isn't that accurate. Now hold on a minute."

"We've got a minute," said Jenny. "But not much more."

"Given all the background, if he's the boss, which I think he is, he has to be American, or anyway live and operate in America."

"Yes."

"An American who can pass as a Frenchman to somebody who knows the language really well."

"Yes."

"And who chooses a wheelchair, of all inconvenient, ostentatious goddam things, to disguise himself in."

"Yes."

184

"What kind of person disguises himself by sitting down all the time?"

"Someone who looks distinguished standing up. I mean distinctive."

The ring of a thousand men began to close, slowly, slowly, on the cemetery. Keeping pace, on the broad smooth track, was the Frenchman's wheelchair.

"Dang my boots," said Colly. "How dumb I have been."

"Now you realize."

"Now I realize. Who, being a trusted business associate, spent a couple of weeks in Dave Cordle's house? With every chance of peeking in his hay store? And knew exactly why I was in New York, and when and where, and where I was going to, and could put a little bomb in Pete's airplane activated by shortwave radio from another airplane? Who employed the guy who reported two deals, both made by men who turned out to be dead?"

"*Capito,*" said Sandro. "Yes, we are dumb."

"*Capito* up to a point," said Jenny. "Bernard Jones located those two men and they both got dead . . . oh. Ah. Good gracious. He got the names of two men who were already dead, and said they were the ones Gabetti had done his deals with?"

"Must be," said Colly.

"There was no other connection at all. They simply had the merit of being dead?"

With an effort Jenny kept her mind on the conversation, diverting it, with an almost physical wrench, from the closing circle of men outside the cemetery walls.

Managing to hold her voice steady, she went on: "And when Bernard Jones was blundering about in Sandro's hospital room—"

"He deposited those little bugs on all of us."

"But I kept my clothes and you lost your clothes. So your friend Mr. Wilkins is a blackmailer?"

"Economic intelligence is a euphemism for industrial espionage, which creates opportunities for blackmail. They have the openings by being on the inside, and they have the gadgetry to capitalize on the openings."

"Very nasty."

"Yes, very. So goddam grateful to Dave Cordle, so solemn and respectful at his funeral, and he was the one who drove the poor guy to death."

"What's odd about his legs?"

"Very short. Born that way, but I don't know why."

"Has he got a grudge because of his funny little legs?"

"Maybe. Or maybe he's just greedy."

The silent ring had advanced, always silent, across the hillside, inwards towards the cemetery. From having been wide apart the men were now close together. Their faces were impassive.

The wheelchair was still part of the advancing line. The valet pushed it at the measured pace of the men of the town. The smooth, pallid face of the man in the wheelchair, behind blue spectacles and under a soft grey hat, was as expressionless as the faces of the townsmen.

"It's nice to know the answer," said Jenny.

"Ma non ci aiuta," said Sandro.

"Not help us?" said Colly. "I think it may, chum. Hand me my walking stick."

Colly struggled to his feet. Sandro handed him the mattock.

"Colly, be careful!" said Jenny in a high, strained voice.

He grinned at her. "Why?"

There was no answer. There was no point in being careful. Any chance, however tiny, however perilous, was worth taking.

Colly limped, very painfully and slowly, to the gate of the cemetery.

Sandro and Jenny followed him to the gate but he motioned them to stop there.

Colly came out of the gate alone.

There was no sound from the men of the town, who stood in a great curved line, shoulder to shoulder, to left and to right.

Colly limped to the wheelchair, until he was a yard away from the thin cotton lap robe which protected the passenger's legs and feet from the dust. The secretary edged up beside his master. The valet kept one hand on the wheelchair and moved the other towards the pocket of his grey cotton coat. The man in the wheelchair put his own hand in his pocket.

The men of the town watched with indifference. They would not be deterred. They would not be much delayed; a slight delay was of no importance.

186

Colly pitched his voice to the most insulting, most arrogantly contemptuous tone.

He said: "Hi, Wilkins, I see you gave up pretending to be a man. I'd ask you to stand up and fight, but as your mother had the syph and produced you like a sawn-off freak. I guess you'll stay in your baby carriage. It's a pity, though. If you stood up you'd give the whole town a laugh."

John Wilkins's face was beginnning to work.

Colly went on, the sneer broadening in his voice: "You did a lot of people a favor, you know that? Remember a girl called Pamela at Oxford? You thought she liked you. She kept a straight face, but boy, when you were out of the room, you should have heard that girl laugh."

John Wilkins's face contorted. His hand came out of his pocket carrying a stubby little .22 automatic. Colly brought the head of the mattock down on his arm. The little gun fell into the dust of the track.

At the same moment the valet drew a heavier pistol. His arm was knocked down by the muzzle of a rifle and he was grabbed by men on each side. The town was not going to be cheated of its execution.

No hand had yet been raised against Colly. The men had advanced no nearer the gate of the cemetery. They showed, in their carved secret faces, no wavering of purpose.

Colly switched to Spanish. He spoke slowly and loudly, so that although he was looking down at John Wilkins many of the men could hear him.

He said: "You are not French and you have no need of that chair. You are an American criminal, about 35 years of age, disguising yourself with white hair and blue spectacles, and disguising the deformity of your ridiculous short legs by sitting down. All this I can and shall prove. You have paid many people to try to kill us because you are too cowardly to do your own killing. Your hirelings broke my leg and my arm, and shot my friends. Now you have tried to trick a whole town into killing us. When I prove to the people of the town that they have been tricked by an American criminal I think they will be very angry. I think they will apologize to me and to my friends, and I think they will hang you and your gang for the bestial and cowardly murder of Ramona Licon. Perhaps your con-

187

temptible deformity has driven you mad. If so you are deserving of God's pity. But you will still be better dead because of the things you have done and the things you will yet do."

There was an enormous silence. The valet was held by the men each side of him. The wheelchair was held by a man of the town. No one had moved.

Colly crossed mental fingers. He ploughed on. He said, more loudly still, and addressing now the lines of silent men to right and left: "I think that a search of your rooms, and of your cars, and of yourself and your friends, will prove what I say. The search will be conducted by the people of the town, perhaps the police, and not by us."

Colly shouted so that as many men as possible could hear him: "We surrender ourselves to the people of the town in the certain knowledge that, at the end of the day, our hands will be shaken in friendship and respect, and your necks will be in the noose which you prepared for us by your lies."

Jenny and Sandro came out of the cemetery. They joined Colly on the broad track in front of the wheelchair. The men formed a dense crowd with a clear space at the center. In the clear space were the wheelchair, the valet and secretary, Colly, Jenny and Sandro.

The crowd walked slowly, always silent, from the cemetery to the town. Sandro supported Colly.

"I hope, darling," murmured Jenny, "you're right about the search."

They did not see the search, nor hear any details of the interrogation which followed it. Neither search nor interrogation was conducted by the police.

The search of the hotel rooms revealed nothing inconsistent with the characters of the Desroches and their servants, except a blonde wig and two large rolls of white webbing bandage. The valet's white coat was not inconsistent with his role, although he had not been seen to wear it in the town.

The search of the cars revealed nothing. They were hired cars, obtained for the party by a travel agent in Mexico City.

What the search and interrogation of the party revealed was not made clear in detail. Nor were the methods of interrogation described. Nothing in the tradition or heredity of the *mestizos* made them likely to be gentle questioners: not the Indian indifference to suffering, the patient stoicism which accepts pain, one's own or another's, as the major part of the human condition: not the Spanish passion for clear-cut unequivocal answers at whatever cost in screams.

The six were taken to the police station, though not by the police, at noon. This was after the blonde wig, the bandages and the white coat had been found. At five in the afternoon Padre Tomas was brought to the station. An hour later the party was brought to the plaza. Their appearance was somewhat changed. The white-haired man in the wheelchair had thin fair hair and he walked, short legged, at the end of a machete. The dark-skinned wife was 30 years younger than she had been before she entered the police station.

Someone, evidently, had made an adequate confession. The Chief of Police was silent. Padre Tomas prayed but did not intervene.

John Wilkins, and his college-educated executives, were hanged in the plaza, six in a row, gently revolving in the evening light, near the bandstand which resembled the frilly paper round a cake.

"But what was it we knew?" asked Jenny, drinking a drink bought for her by the town.

"That's the final irony," said Colly. "We knew nothing."

Jenny and Sandro both looked at him blankly.

"When I went to see John Wilkins in New York, they left me alone in his office. A girl came in with some files on the case, and they still left me alone. I should think they dumped her in an acid bath after I left. And they put a little bomb in Pete's airplane. And all the rest when that didn't work."

"What do you suppose was in the files?"

"Might be a lot of things. A copy of a letter they wrote to Gabetti. A letter from a bank showing they were the Blue Hill Pilgrims. The letter they sent to Dave Cordle. The report Bernard Jones really put in. Any of those might have put me wise, or halfway wise."

"But you didn't peek at the files."

"Of course not."

"But Wilkins thought you did."

"Yeah. *He* would have peeked, being a natural-born peeker. It never crossed his mind that a guy, ah, a little better brought up, might simply *not* steal a look at somebody else's confidential papers."

"If he did not suspect you wrongly," said Sandro slowly, "he would be alive tonight, and in New York, and making millions of dollars by blackmail."

"Undone by his own nasty mind," said Jenny. "The very thought gives me a thirst."

"Anche me," said Sandro.

The town was proud to slake their thirst.